COMPLICIT

ALSO BY STEPHANIE KUEHN

CHARM & STRANGE
DELICATE MONSTERS

COMPLICIT

STEPHANIE KUEHN

ST. MARTIN'S GRIFFIN ⚞ NEW YORK

COMPLICIT. Copyright © 2014 by Stephanie Kuehn. All rights reserved. Printed in the United States of America. For information, address St. Martin's Press, 175 Fifth Avenue, New York, N.Y. 10010.

www.stmartins.com

Designed by Anna Gorovoy

The Library of Congress has cataloged the hardcover edition as follows:

Kuehn, Stephanie.
    Complicit / Stephanie Kuehn. — First edition.
        p. cm.
    ISBN 978-1-250-04459-4 (hardcover)
    ISBN 978-1-4668-4305-9 (e-book)
    1. Mental illness—Fiction.   2. Amnesia—Fiction.   3. Brothers and sisters—Fiction.   4. Private schools—Fiction.   5. Schools—Fiction.   6. Orphans—Fiction.   I. Title.
    PZ7.K94872Com 2014
    [Fic]—dc23

                                                    2014008117

ISBN 978-1-250-04460-0 (trade paperback)

Our books may be purchased in bulk for promotional, educational, or business use. Please contact your local bookseller or the Macmillan Corporate and Premium Sales Department at (800) 221-7945, extension 5442, or by e-mail at Macmillan SpecialMarkets@macmillan.com.

First St. Martin's Griffin Trade Paperback Edition: March 2016

10   9   8   7   6   5   4   3   2   1

For every truth best left a lie

1

EVIDENCE

ONE

My phone is ringing.

It's 3:29.

In the *morning*.

The phone keeps ringing. Or not ringing really—the Monk song I have programmed is what's playing, and the notes, the beat, sound sort of sad, sort of mournful, against the bleak-black December night. I groan and fumble around in the sheets. I like to be prepared, so I sleep with my phone beneath my pillow just in case someone calls. No one ever does, of course.

Except for now.

More fumbling, but my fingers find the phone at last. I slide it out and hold it in front of my face. My eyes are bleary and my brain slow, but what I'm seeing on the touch screen finally registers:

Unknown caller.

Okay.

I answer.

"Hello?" I say.

Nothing. I hear nothing.

"Who is this?"

No response, but I press the phone closer to my ear. No one speaks, but I hear something. I do. Short feral bursts of noise. Organic. Like a faint sobbing.

Or laughing.

"Hey," I say, a little louder than before. I want to make sure that I'm heard. "I know you're there. Who're you trying to reach?"

Still no answer, and nothing keeps happening, the way nothing sometimes does. The phone line remains open, and I remain listening. The human sounds fade. They're replaced by a howling wind. The muffled blare of a horn.

I lay my head against my pillow and look up at the ceiling, shadowy and dark. Outside the house, rain falls softly. This is December in California. The phone beeps that its battery is low, but I don't move. Instead I close my eyes, and on the backs of my lids, I picture places where the wind might be blowing.

The desert.

The mountains.

The ragged edge of the world.

I still don't move.

I fall asleep with the phone against my ear.

"Jamie," Angie says to me at breakfast the next morning. "We thought you should hear it from us first."

"Hear what, Mom?" I ask. I call Angie Mom because that's what she likes and because it's so rarely the thought that counts. That's dishonest on my part, I know, but if I had to pick one quality to define me, it's this—I can't stand to hurt other people's feelings. Not saying what I mean is sometimes the best way I know how to be kind.

From the other side of the kitchen, Angie's husband Malcolm straightens his silk tie and pours coffee into his stainless-steel travel mug. He only drinks the organic free trade stuff, which is expensive as hell, but, hey, Malcolm can definitely afford it. He even grinds the beans at home. Like it's some kind of virtue.

"It's your sister," he says.

I stiffen. "My sister?"

"Yes."

"What about her?"

"She's been released."

My hands go ice-cold the way they always do when I'm taken by surprise.

This is not a good thing.

"Are you okay?" Angie asks as my fork clatters to the hardwood floor. Maple syrup dots the front of my T-shirt and jeans on the way down.

"But I thought—"

"We thought the same thing." Malcolm fits the lid just right onto his mug. *Click.* He hasn't noticed my hands yet. They're completely numb now and useless. I look down at my food, cut-up whole-grain waffles that I can no longer eat, and sort of jam my arms into my lap. It can take hours to get feeling back, a whole day even—some kind of nerve thing that even the big-shot doctors down at Stanford can't figure out after years of rigorous and invasive testing. I shake my head and try to keep breathing. This is so not what I needed.

Not now.

Not when I have a full day of classes, including AP physics and digital arts.

Not when I play piano in the school jazz band and we have our winter performance tonight at the civic auditorium in downtown Danville.

Not when Jenny Lacouture and I are supposed to hang out together at lunch and I've been trying for weeks to get up the nerve to ask her out on a real date.

Just not . . . not *Cate*.

My throat goes dry.

Is *she* the one who called last night?

"She wasn't supposed to get out until June," I say, and I instantly regret my tone. This isn't Angie and Malcolm's fault. This is not what they want, either. God knows.

"Your hands," Angie says. "I'll call your doctor."

"No, don't. Please. I can do that myself."

Her lips tighten to a line. "I'll get your gloves, then."

I give what I hope is a grateful nod, and as Angie hustles from the room, there's still a spring in her step. Taking care of me is what she does best.

I turn and look back at Malcolm. His gray hair. His stoic face. That damn silk tie.

"She got out early," he says, and I can sense he feels just as helpless as I do. "Two weeks ago. Good behavior or overcrowding or something."

"Why didn't someone tell us?"

"Cate's nineteen now. No one has to tell us anything."

"Then how'd you find out?"

Angie sweeps back in. She's preceded by the smell of gardenias, which is the perfume she always wears and the one that always gives me a headache. She's waving a pair of my dumb gloves around, but there's a look that passes between her and Malcolm—one forged from wide eyes and knowing nods. It's the one they share when they think I can't handle things and the one that means they're keeping secrets. I feel the urge to call them on it, to demand an answer, but I don't want to upset them, either. Not upsetting people is sort of the modus operandi around here.

After Cate, it's a welcome change.

"Where is she?" I ask.

"Far away," Angie says. She picks up my left hand and forces on the first leather shearling-lined glove. My fingers bend every which way with the effort. It's sort of sickening to watch, but I let her do it. Everyone says heat is good for circulation, only I've never been able to tell that it helps any.

"Far away," I echo, as Angie straightens up and brushes hair from my eyes. It used to be blond, my hair, but now it's aged into the same light brown as hers. Like a chameleon's trick—familial camouflage.

"She's got no reason to come back here, James. None. We've seen the last of her."

I nod again. This is a sentiment I'd like to believe, but I don't. There are things I know about my sister that no one else does. Bad things. Things I can't say. Not without hurting Angie and Malcolm or causing them grief, and I don't have it in me to do that. So instead, I lift my chin and smile warmly at my adoptive parents. This is good, reassuring. My actions send the message that I'm fine, totally fine.

I'm not fine, of course. Not even close.

But like I said, it's so rarely the thought that counts.

TWO

The last night I saw Cate, she was drunk. Or on drugs. Or just plain crazy.

Take your pick.

I snuck into her room on the eve of her sentencing. It was close to midnight. None of her lights were on, but a full moon spilled a silvery wash across the floorboards, the far wall.

I huddled at the foot of her bed, like a rodent in sawdust.

I was scared.

"You shouldn't be here," she told me.

My chest hiccupped, once, twice. I was filled not only with fear, but that unbearable sting of sadness and grief: I was losing my sister.

In truth, she'd been lost for some time now, but I didn't want her to go. Only she'd caused so much pain, she didn't deserve to stay.

I knew that.

And it made me sad.

Forcing down the lump rising in my throat, I whispered, "Why'd you do it?"

Cate snorted. "Oh, so you think I did it now, do you? You think I'm guilty?"

"Well, I guess . . . well, you pleaded guilty, didn't you? That's what the judge said."

"Fuck you, Jamie! Just fuck you! You're like all the rest of them!"

"Shhh!" Her anger scraped my nerves. "Stop screaming, all right!"

My sister leaped from her bed and spun herself toward the window. She wore hardly anything the way she always did. Just panties and some sheer top. I turned away and didn't look. I didn't dare. I was fourteen. She was sixteen. I *knew* better.

"If you didn't do it, then who did?" I asked, my face still staring at the wall. Actually I was staring at a poster of Anne Parillaud from *La Femme Nikita*. It was hard not to. Those lips. Those eyes.

That gun.

From across the room, I heard the sharp *flick-whoosh* and hiss of a butane lighter. The sound chilled me. It set my hands tingling. It reminded me of my own secret. The one I'd vowed not to tell, but knew I'd never forget. Cate took a deep inhale of whatever it was she was smoking, then blew it all back into the night like a promise. "Oh, right, little brother. You're real good, you know that?"

"Good at what?" I asked.

She laughed loudly, her throaty voice deeper and more cutting than it'd ever been. "Acting like you don't know anything."

THREE

After breakfast, Angie drops me off at school. I hate it. The being dropped off, that is, not school. I got my real license last month when I turned seventeen, no more provisional, and the Henrys gave me my own car to mark the occasion. That's nice, I know. Beyond nice. I have a good life with them, and I try to remember that.

The car they bought me is a Jeep, black, this year's model, and I'm kind of in love with it. It's got a moon roof. Satellite radio. Leather seats and trim. Way more than I ever could've dreamed of. So much so, I feel a little like an impostor behind the wheel. But I've taken to calling the Jeep Dr. No, which pleases me in ways I wouldn't confess to under torture. The only thing I worry about is having one of my nerve attacks while driving. I'd probably fly off the road and into a tree if that happened. None of my doctors seem particularly concerned, though. I haven't had an episode this bad in over a year, and they signed off on my papers for the DMV and everything. Maybe that'll change now. I don't know. Maybe I just worry more than other people.

Today, obviously, Dr. No's been left sleeping in the Henrys' three-car garage on the other side of town, and instead of parking myself in the student lot and walking to class like everyone else, I'm getting helped out of Angie's Volvo and dumped onto the front lawn of Sayrebrook Academy like an invalid. People are staring and everything, which I resent, but what can you do?

Somehow we're running late, and I have to sprint through the halls to get to first period English on time. Angie heads to the main office to explain what's going on with my hands. She'll also let them know I'm going to need an aide for the day, which won't be too big a deal. Sayrebrook's an elite school. It costs like twenty grand a year to go here, so they're usually pretty accommodating when I need extra help. But I always feel awful for asking. Even though it doesn't have anything to do with *me*, my family doesn't have the greatest reputation around here.

I make it, barely, sliding my ass into my first-row seat at the exact moment the tardy bell rings. Mr. O'Meara nods at the class, and everyone takes out their laptops.

Except me.

"I'll need to use the voice recognition today," I say in my most apologetic voice, and if anyone's rolling their eyes behind my back or flipping me off, well, I wouldn't know because I've gotten used to tuning that kind of thing out. It's all about tunnel vision.

"That's fine, Jamie." Mr. O'Meara gestures toward the opposite side of the room. "Why don't you sit in the back where you won't disturb the other students. We'll be working on the theory papers this morning. You'll find a graded first draft in your folder."

"Sure thing," I say. One of the OT aides from the disability office comes in and helps me get set up. I relax a little. This is good. I need to work on this paper. It's the one I want to use so that I can apply to the cognitive science program over at Berkeley next summer. A whole four-week session, and I'd get to live in the dorms and everything. It'd sure be a nice escape from reality (and no, the irony of that thought is not lost on me), but to get in, I first have to write an essay on a philosophical issue. The one I've chosen to write about is fate, because it's something I believe in. You know, that our destiny lives inside of us. I think we're born with it, what we're meant to do with our lives. It's just up to us to find out what that is.

I look over Mr. O'Meara's notes. They're mostly positive, but he's telling me to go deeper, which is what he always tells us: *Go deeper. Don't be afraid to get your hands dirty.* Well, I can't do anything with my hands right now, so his figure of speech falls flat for me today. I quickly read over the rest of what he's written. Most of my paper is on Plato and Aristotle, but my teacher's suggested a bunch of other reading, like Emerson. Nietzsche. Sartre. I open the links he's given me and browse the online library. The texts he wants me to read look seriously dense.

I can't deal.

Soon my mind wanders. I let my gaze drift out the window, at tree-dotted hills, at black crows and tule fog. My eyelids droop. That phone call in the middle of the night has exhausted me. Not only that, it's disturbed me.

I have no proof it was Cate who called, but what if? My sister's spent the last two years in a juvenile detention center in Southern California, locked up in a place where the sun always shines and there's not much else worth mentioning. Where would she go? Los Angeles? Vegas? I don't know. But I can definitely see her calling me on a throwaway phone in the dead of night. That'd be Cate all the way. I envision her standing on the side of the road, maybe outside some seedy truck stop in the middle of nowhere, thumb outstretched. Her jeans too tight. Her shirt too low. Her mood too black.

Just asking for trouble.

I take a deep breath. Not that Cate's ever done the right thing, but she wouldn't dare come back here. There's nothing for her in Danville. Well, nothing good. She knows that.

She *has* to.

Right?

FOUR

My sister Cate and I come from humble beginnings.

Our real mother's name was Amy Nevin, and she grew up in the backwoods of Oregon in a town known for nothing but logging, devout Christianity, and abject poverty. I've never seen a picture of her, but sometimes it *feels* like I have, as if her memories and life experiences were transferred to me along with her DNA. At times, it's like I can close my eyes and soften my mind and see a tall girl with hollow shoulders and black hair sitting on the steps to a trailer. She's bored. She's restless. She's miserable. Cate told me Amy ran away from home when she was sixteen. This could be true. It could be something Cate made up.

I have no way of knowing.

Amy hitched her way to San Francisco. Cate thinks she got pregnant on the way down here, lifting her skirt as payment for miles, for comfort, for survival, I don't know. For my part, I don't like to think about that. It's just as likely she was already knocked up when she left, or maybe it happened when she got to California and discovered San Francisco was way too expensive for a teenage girl with no diploma and no money. She ended up across the Bay in Richmond's Iron Triangle with some guy named Albert who worked nights cleaning bathrooms at the local junior college. Albert deserted for points unknown on the day Cate was born, which doesn't prove he wasn't her father.

It only proves he didn't want to be.

My own paternity is equally a mystery. I don't like to think about that, either. For almost six years, I lived with my mom and my sister in the basement of a drafty house surrounded on three sides by railroad tracks and not-so-quiet desperation. My memories of my mother are faint and few and far between, but the ones I do have can wake me up at night with their strength. Out of nowhere they come to me, pure sensory overload blowing in like gale-force winds to shatter my bones and break my heart: the sweet, sweet scent of cigarettes on her clothes. The primal warmth of the bed we shared, me on one side of her, Cate snoring on the other. The soft way her long dark hair tickled my face when she wanted me to laugh. It's easier to remember the good than the bad, I guess, but sometimes I can't help but remember other things, too, like the drugs and the men and her moods and being hungry and not having jackets when the weather turned cold. I loved her, though.

Deeply. Madly.

She was *mine*.

What I don't remember is the day she died. We saw it all, I guess, but in an act of mercy, my brain has rejected those moments. Forever. I do know she was shot by an intruder. Multiple times. Blood gurgled out of her, and my twenty-four-year-old mother died slumped against the wall near the bed where we all slept. Cate says she held me in her arms until it was over. She didn't want me to see what she saw.

Then she called 911.

The time right after our mother's death is a blur for me. Malcolm and Angie and Cate have helped me piece it together after the fact, but all I can recall is darkness and sorrow and a deep, deep well of pain.

I wanted her back.

I cried.

And I wanted her back.

We were placed in emergency foster care. Then we were placed in a group home. We had case managers and new schools and new teachers and people who tried to track down relatives willing to take us. There were none. At the home I pined and ate nothing. I refused to go to school and got sick when I had to. My only attachments were to my sister and a filthy silk blanket square I'd taken to calling Pinky. Cate did what she could, but it wasn't enough. I grew bony and pale and picked up lice and a lisp and a bad habit of pulling out my eyebrows that made me look odd and somewhat slow. When the Henrys agreed to take both of us, no one was more surprised than our social worker.

Miss Louise, of the permed hair, cat's-eye glasses, and heavy makeup, smoked menthol cigarettes on the car ride over. "I know I told you how hard it is to keep families together. Especially at your age. But Malcolm and Angie specifically requested a brother and sister who were both in grade school. Guess they must want to skip over the diaper-and-tantrum stage, huh?"

Cate giggled and held my hand. I desperately clutched Pinky in the other.

It turned out the Henrys didn't want to skip over anything. They'd already been through the diaper-and-tantrum stage with their own two children: Madison and Graham, who'd both been killed instantly in a tragic traffic accident involving malfunctioning railway signals. Their ages at death: nine and six.

Cate and I were meant to fit right in.

The Henrys gave us everything. They had the money for it. Danville was one of the richest towns on the outskirts of the San Francisco Bay Area, nestled far to the east in a stretch of rolling California hills and mossy live oaks. We lived in a mansion, behind iron gates. We had our own rooms and our own toys, and we swam in a black-bottomed pool with a waterfall that overlooked ranch land and steep winding trails. Cate got a pony. I got piano lessons. We went to an esteemed private academy meant to nurture our individual talents.

Twin losses brought us together. Made us a family.

Almost.

FIVE

I know that guys my age usually look to athletes like LeBron or Brady or Lincecum for inspiration, but the person I admire most has got to be jazz pianist Thelonious Monk. Maybe that makes me weird or pretentious or whatever, but his music is the one thing in life that can make me feel relevant and make me feel free. Monk wasn't afraid to be different, you know? He cut right through what other people called dissonance, and he played *outside* the chords. That kind of vision takes guts.

It's also the kind of vision I'm wishing I had during the morning break at school. That's when I catch sight of Jenny Lacouture standing by her locker in the hallway. Her soft blond hair's pulled off her neck, and her slim legs are bare beneath her plaid skirt. We've been spending a lot of time together lately, Jenny and I, so I'd like to think she's standing there on purpose, just hoping I'll notice her.

How could I not?

I walk over to her with butterflies flapping inside of me, good ones, the kind that make me feel like I could float. Jenny's a junior like I am, and she plays piano, too, which is sort of perfect. Techniquewise, she might even be better than me, but that's a lot harder to admit than it probably should be.

"I'm not holding your hand today," I tell her.

Jenny's brown eyes go wide, and I can almost hear the wheels turning inside her head as she tries to figure out if I mean what I say. I do, of course, just not in the way she thinks.

"It's my nerve thing," I confess. "I've told you about that, haven't I?"

She looks down to see the gloves, the way my arms are sort of cradled against my stomach.

"Oh," she says. "What happened?"

"They went numb this morning. At breakfast."

"But you'll be okay?"

"I should be."

"What's it called again?"

"The neurologist thinks it's a form of cataplexy, but that's usually only seen with narcolepsy, and I don't fall asleep in weird places or anything. So it's idiopathic."

"What does that word mean?" she asks. "Idiopathic?"

"It means they don't know why it happens." I roll my shoulders and force a bland expression on my face. I don't tell Jenny about the other theory I have, the more embarrassing one: that it's all in my mind, that my hands going numb is some sort of anxiety symptom, set off by high levels of stress and my basic inability to *deal*.

Luckily Jenny doesn't ask more questions. Instead she presses her lips together and smiles that smile I like so much, the one that's crooked and honest all at once.

"I've seen you fall asleep in class before," she says. "You're kind of cute when you sleep, Jamie Henry. I think I'd like it if you had that narcolepsy thing."

I try smiling back, but it's weird. Sometimes the things Jenny says are so nice they can make me feel sad. Like right now. It's my own personal paradox, I guess—either my brain doesn't know how to be happy or my heart doesn't know how to let me.

"I'd like it, too, if it meant being able to see your face when I woke up," I say softly.

Hector Ramirez makes a barfing sound as he walks past us. "Jesus. What the fuck is this shit? A Disney movie? Just hump already and get it over with."

"Shut up," I snap. Goddamn Hector. Jenny shouldn't have to hear crap like that. Ever. Unfortunately, I can't flip him off.

Hector pauses. "So is it true?" he asks me.

"Is what true?"

"That Cate's out."

I tense. "Where'd you hear that?"

He lifts a dark eyebrow. "So it *is* true? Damn. That's one rumor I didn't want to believe, Henry. You know why. Crazy Cate."

"Where'd you hear about Cate?" I repeat, although I think I might know.

Hector throws his hands in the air, feigning ignorance, and begins walking backward. "Dunno, man. Nowhere. Somewhere. Anywhere. But your sister's a bad girl. Bad, bad, bad. The worst, even. So you tell her she can come see me, and we can talk face-to-face if she's got a problem with my family this time. Tell her she doesn't have to—"

"Stop," I say weakly. "I'm not telling her anything, okay? I haven't even *talked* to her. You probably know more than I do."

"You have a sister?" Jenny asks, and a loose strand of hair dances across her collarbone in a way that entrances me. Like it's got a mind of its own.

"Yes," I say, pulling my gaze away. "Hector, you need to tell me what you heard."

Jenny touches my shoulder. "Where's your sister coming back from?"

"Jail," I say, then: "I'm serious, Hector!"

"I'm serious, too," he yells. Then he's gone. Swallowed up by the crowd.

I turn back to Jenny. There're people all around us, jostling, shouting, shoving, but she's looking at me with concern. *Me.*

I take a deep breath.

I push down the sad feeling in my heart.

"Jenny," I say. "Would you go out with me Friday night?"

"Yes." She answers without hesitation, and right then my hands come back to life. Like magic.

I show her.

"Look at that." I wiggle my fingers.

"So you're all right?"

"More than all right. You did that."

The look on her face is cautious. "I did?"

"Oh, sure," I say earnestly. "You're like my sun in winter."

SIX

There are no coincidences in life. That's part of believing in fate, I guess. I also think *fate* is different from *faith,* although sometimes it's hard for me to explain why, which is probably the reason I haven't been able to get out of going to church on Sundays. Either way, it still makes sense to me that the first time I went numb was when I heard about what Cate did.

It happened more than two years ago now, in early October. I was a freshman sitting in the well-landscaped quad of Sayrebrook Academy, killing time before class. Actually, I was trying to cram for a science exam, but that wasn't such an easy task to complete while the varsity cheerleaders practiced their pom-pomming not twenty feet from where

I sat. In addition to their short-short skirts, they brought a savagery to their shaking that was difficult to ignore. Finally I squeezed my eyes shut, as hard as I could, and went over the biology terms I'd been studying:

Neuron
Dendrite
Axon
Synapse
Neurotransmitter
Action potential

"Open your eyes," a voice whispered right in my ear, and I ducked to one side, annoyed. But I didn't obey. I didn't have to; I recognized both my best friend Scooter's voice and his lame movie quote. I hated *Vanilla Sky,* and he knew it.

"Go away," I said, swatting at him like I would a bug.

"Why?"

"I'm studying."

"You're always studying, Henry. Where's it ever gotten you?"

"I'm not worried about where it's *gotten* me. I'm worried about where I'm going. And you should, too, unless you don't mind living in your stepmom's basement for the next twenty years."

"Ouch," Scooter said. Then: "Oh, shit, look at that."

"Is it that goth chick again? I told you I don't think she's—"

"No, dude. It's *cops.*"

I opened my eyes.

On the far side of the quad by the admin building, no less than four city police cars sat parked, lights flashing but not making any noise. The cops themselves stood talking with a group of adults. I could see the principal, Mrs. Watkins, and at least two of the school guidance counselors.

"What's going on?" Scooter breathed.

Two girls ran past us then, straight up to the cheerleaders, who'd paused in their pom-pomming to watch the scene.

"It's Sarah Ciorelli!" one of the girls cried out.

Scooter gasped.

My head turned.

Sarah?

"She's in the hospital! They don't know if she'll make it!"

Then it seemed like everyone was screaming. The news traveled fast, racing across campus as if tragedy had its own action potential: Fourteen-year-old freshman Sarah Ciorelli had been badly hurt in a midnight fire that destroyed one of the main barns on the prestigious Ramirez ranch property. It's where she, and a lot of Danville residents, my own family members included, boarded their fancy show horses.

And Sarah was Scooter's girlfriend.

My books tumbled to the ground. Lined paper notes fluttered from my grasp.

"Scooter!"

"What?" He had his phone out, frantically texting. His cheeks had gone red, his eyes wild.

"I can't feel my hands," I said. By now the wind was scattering my papers across the courtyard. They danced and twirled in the sky like sad flakes of snow too stupid to know they didn't belong.

"I don't care about your hands, man! This is *Sarah* we're talking about. It must be some kind of mistake. It has to be. I don't get why she'd—"

"I'm fucking serious!"

Scooter blinked, startled. I rarely swore. He finally looked at me, gasping and hunched over with arms that hung limp and lifeless like they were made of wood. "Huh?"

"I can't feel anything. It's my hands. They're *numb*."

SEVEN

I'm in gym when Cate calls. Even though I've been excused for the day, Coach Marks, the PE teacher, insists on making me change clothes. It's a dick move on his part, but whatever. A lot of people don't like me on account of what my sister did, and I can't do anything to fix that. So this is the reason I'm sitting in the corner, alone, squeezed into a pair of green athletic shorts and a white Sayrebrook Academy shirt that's at least two sizes too small, while everyone else does Pilates on the yoga room floor. *Pilates.* It probably comes as no surprise that sports aren't really my thing, so gym clothes or not, I just thank God I'm not having to flop around on a faded foam exercise mat, showing off my lack of core strength or something.

I sneak a glance at my phone once the class is done with warm-ups. I'm hoping to see a message from Jenny, although I know it's unlikely. She's got this thing about texting at school that I'm trying not to take personally. Some promise she's made to her mom. I tell her I understand, but the truth is, I don't. Not really.

That's when I see it. Not a text: a voice mail. From an unlisted number. My ringer's off, which is how I missed the call, but deep down, I sort of expected this. That's part of fate or karma or kismet, isn't it? Getting what you deserve.

Well, I definitely deserve this.

Hey, Jamie babe. I know you know who this is. I know you know other things, too. So maybe it won't come as a surprise when I tell you I'll be coming back to Danville soon, and that the person I want to see most is you. Then again, I've been wrong before, haven't I? So why don't you go ahead and consider this fair warning . . .

"Hey! *Hey!*"

Someone's yelling at me, and I can't answer them. I can't answer because I'm standing in the locker room with my head stuck beneath the sink faucet, and my heart's pounding so fast it feels like a runaway truck. It feels like my brakes have gone out. It feels like—

Like I can't *breathe.*

"Jamie, hey! You all right, man?"

Water is pouring down the back of my neck, my shirt.

Someone shakes me.

"Hey!"

Whoever it is shakes harder, then grabs on to my collar. I'm yanked upright. My hair's matted flat. Water streams into my eyes.

"I'm fine!" I gasp. "Seriously."

I blink until I can see. Nick Hsu, a senior, is holding me at arm's length. His face reflects irritation. Confusion, too, along with a good helping of contempt. I've seen it all before, though. Nick's not the first person to look at me that way.

I take a deep breath. Feel my heartbeat start to slow. I've had plenty of panic attacks before, but this was different. This one was bad. My hands are tingling like crazy, but they haven't gone numb, which is a relief. I couldn't deal with the paralysis again so soon.

"You sure you're okay?" Nick releases me and takes a step backward. "You ran out of that gym like your ass was on fire. Coach made me come see what's up."

"Yeah. Sorry. I'm okay now."

"Well, here you go." He holds something out.

It's my phone. I take it from him, and that's when it comes back to me. Sort of. I still don't remember getting from the gym to the locker room, but I do remember what it was that set off my anxiety. It wasn't Cate's voice. It was her *words*.

Her threat.

"Thanks," I say, but I feel sick all over again.

Cate's coming back to Danville.

For *me*.

EIGHT

After school I have to take the bus to see my therapist, Dr. Waverly. She might be a shrink, actually, not a therapist. I'm not sure. She's the kind of doctor that can give you medication, but she also likes to talk about my feelings.

So maybe she's both.

I get off at my stop in Danville Village at ten to three, which gives me enough time to walk the rest of the way. I skirt sidewalk puddles and rich ladies pushing strollers. This is a real upscale part of town, and instead of regular square buildings, all the businesses here live and breathe inside Victorian row houses. One of them is Dr. Waverly's, and I could probably find it in my sleep, that's how well I know the place.

Maybe that's not such a great thing to admit, but I'm not certifiable or anything like that. It's just, after what happened with our mom, I had issues with worrying. I like to think that's normal.

The ironic thing is, when we first moved in with the Henrys, *Cate* was the well-adjusted one. Cate was everything then. At eight years old, she was precocious. Outgoing. Spunky. She took to Angie in an instant, slipping into poor dead Madison's rich-girl role like an understudy. I was pretty much her polar opposite, and my problems became glaringly obvious on the day Grammy and Grandpa Karlsson, Angie's parents, came to visit all the way from Sweden for our first summer with the family.

At that point, we'd only been with the Henrys for seven weeks.

At that point, our mother had only been dead for seven months.

At the airport, Cate bounced and ran straight for our new grandfather. She wrapped her arms around him. Legs, too.

"Well, well," he said, squeezing her hard. Cate wouldn't let go. "She's a friendly one, isn't she? Run right into the arms of Charles Manson, this one would."

Grammy Karlsson, who was shaky and mean-looking, peered down at me over the rims of her bifocals and said, "What's wrong with his face?"

I cowered. A lot was wrong with my face. My eyebrows were still gone, and in addition to being gaunt and sickly and practically hairless, I cried way too much, at the drop of a hat, an act that left my eyes pink and puffy like a lab rat's. Nothing made me happy. Not the niceness of Angie and Malcolm. Not the vibrant spirit of my sister. Instead, my well of sorrow grew deeper and wider with each passing day. I got picked on in school for my lisp. I wouldn't talk or do my work. I worried about monsters. I worried about planes hitting our house. I worried about people breaking in and killing everyone. I worried *I* would go crazy and kill everyone. I had nightmares about blood and more blood and death and body parts and loss and terror and I was scared.

All the time.

Of everything.

"He's a good boy. He's just . . . still adjusting," Angie told her mother. "Go on, Jamie. Hold Grammy's hand." She nudged me forward. I stumbled and my stomach cramped like I might get sick, which I knew would be bad, but I did what I was told.

Grammy's hand felt brittle and papery to me. Stale. She reminded me of an old art project, constructed from paste and macaroni wheels. We walked together from baggage claim, and she asked me questions like did they have manners where I came from and why did I still talk baby talk and did I know how lucky I was to have been taken in by such a wealthy family? I felt my own non-stale hand grow clammy and wet, like overripe fruit. I wanted to wipe it on my pants, but didn't dare let go. I didn't dare do anything that might come off as rude.

Making our way down a long flight of steps toward the airport parking lot, Grandpa and Cate skipped ahead, chatting cheerily. I took each step with great care, still holding on to Grammy while at the same time trying very hard not to throw up on my shoes.

"Hey!" Grammy said, yanking on my shoulder socket. "Pay attention!"

I blinked and looked up. "Huh?"

"Are you even listening to me?"

"N-no. I'm sorry," I said, but with the way I talked back then, it sounded like *tharry*.

She pursed her old-lady lips. "Angie says you won't call her Mom yet, but you will soon, won't you?"

My shoulders rolled in a listless shrug.

"You'll forget all about that other woman. I know you will. She sounds absolutely frightful!"

Suddenly my head swam with dizziness. I ripped my hand from hers.

"What's wrong with you?" Grammy asked.

"My mother's not frightful!" I shouted. "She's not!"

She smirked. "That's not what I heard. Living in filth. Having babies on her own. You're better off now. You just don't know it."

My blood boiled. I wanted to yell at her more, to say something awful, something *more* than awful, but I didn't. I couldn't. My tongue stuck to the roof of my mouth, and my vocal cords wouldn't work.

Grammy kept talking, shaking her finger, too, but my ears weren't working, either. I couldn't hear what she said. I couldn't hear anything. Instead I took a step backward. I felt myself trip and fall.

And fall.

I kept falling. Like a dry leaf in autumn.

Then everything around me went dark.

Hours later, when I opened my eyes, I was in the children's hospital with a green cast on my left arm and Cate looking right at me. She had a huge grin on her face. Freckles dotted her nose. She'd taken in sun lately. Me, I hurt all over. Everywhere.

"That was so cool," she said.

"What was so cool?"

"You." She shoved Pinky into my lap. I slipped the silk edge of the blanket square into the webbed space between my thumb and forefinger on my good hand, and began sliding it back and forth.

"Me?" I asked.

She nodded. "You fell down, like, a whole flight of steps at the airport. It was awesome. Like a movie stunt!"

"I fell?"

"Grammy Karlsson said you got so upset you held your breath on purpose."

"What? No I didn't!"

"Uh-huh. Yes you did." Cate played with her hair. It was different from mine: black, shiny, flowing past her shoulders. "Grammy said you held it until you *fainted*. She thinks you're totally nuts. Told Angie to send you back and everything, but I said I'd help take care of you. She likes me."

My heart beat way too fast. "Why can't I remember that?"

"Those people in the ambulance. They gave you pills right after. Something for the pain." Her voice lowered. "You were really screaming something awful, Jamie. But they said the pills would make you forget what happened. Probably a good thing, don't ya think?"

After I got out of the hospital, I went to see Dr. Waverly for the first time. I was shy and didn't want to, but Malcolm convinced me she wasn't the type of doctor who gave shots or reset bones. And he was right. All we did that first time was talk. Dr. Waverly sat across from me and told me that years ago she and her partner had adopted a baby boy from Guatemala, and that she liked helping children who were going through similar transitions. Her disclosure about her son made me feel safe. And understood. We also talked about other things, like holding my breath until I passed out. I told her I didn't do that, but that no one believed me. Dr. Waverly said she believed me. I told her I was mad about what Grammy Karlsson had said about my real mom, and she said she believed that, too.

I liked her.

The second time I saw her, Dr. Waverly asked if I would do a bunch of tests with her. I said I would, and the tests we did were fun, not just the kind where you had to prove you knew different letters and numbers. These were ones where I got to play games and make drawings of myself with my new family. She also wanted me to look at pictures and make up stories about them.

"And what might this be?" she'd ask, holding up an inkblot card.

I'd stare and stare. Answering took me a long time because I wanted so badly to be *right*. "It's a monster. A scary monster. And he's angry, you can tell because he has these streaks of red that show off his anger. He wants to kill someone. That's why his boots are so big. So the police can't find out who he is."

At the end of it all, she told me I had severe anxiety, and that the reason I couldn't remember my mother dying was because of something called dissociative amnesia. She explained that my brain was so smart and so special it had found a way to forget the trauma. Only my body was still scared. That's why I worried so much. She said she wanted to help me be less anxious, that there were pills she could give me and things we could do together, but that more than anything, I had to want to help myself.

I cried.

I said I wanted help.

I wish Cate had gotten help, too.

NINE

Dr. Waverly's office door swings open just as the hour hand hits three. I jump up from the waiting room couch, and she waves me in, shutting the door behind me.

"How's school, Jamie?" she asks, because I have my backpack with me. It's the same black JanSport I've been dragging around since ninth grade—worn spots, pencil holes, ink stains, and all. Angie's tried throwing it away on more than one occasion, but I keep rescuing it from the trash.

"I'm doing pretty good," I tell her.

"Still top of the honor roll?"

"Yup. Almost all AP classes this semester, too." My cheeks burn a little as I say this, because it sounds like bragging, but I've worked hard on Accepting My Strengths this past year. I don't want to sell myself short.

Dr. Waverly smiles in response. She's big on the positive reinforcement thing. "Plus jazz band. Plus that cognitive science program you're applying to. You're a very accomplished student."

Quick nod, but then I duck my head. Hell, there's only so much self-praise a guy can take. Walking over to the window, I flop down in my usual chair—soft calfskin leather—and try to get comfortable. I'm not particularly tall or built, but I like to spread out when I'm here, to give the illusion of mass. Dr. Waverly would call that a defense mechanism, I guess. She says I have a lot of those. She also says they're healthy.

I do my usual scan of the room. It's important to me that things don't change in this office. I've been seeing Dr. Waverly on and off for a long time now, since I was a kid, and I figure if you're going to make the effort to depend on someone who gets paid to be your friend, the least they can do is be consistent. And she is. She's always had the same framed Monet hanging on the eastern wall. The same Navajo rug spread on the floor between us. The only additions to this space over the years have been comforting ones: a stone owl with crystal eyes that sits and watches me from its perch on the windowsill; a photo of her son on the day he graduated from medical school, cap in hand, face beaming with pride. Plus there are always precisely five clocks in this room. I count every time. The smallest, made of brushed steel, sits on the bookcase to my left. It faces away from me, but I can still hear the racing heartbeat of our fifty-minute hour tick, tick, ticking away.

"How're you handling things?" Dr. Waverly asks.

I tap my fingers. "Okay."

"You have gloves on."

"I know."

"Does that mean—"

"Yeah. I had one of my nerve attacks this morning. A bad one. First time in a while."

Her brows pop up over her glasses. "Bad?"

"It lasted until right before lunch. So not the worst, but . . . you know."

"That sounds pretty bad."

I nod.

She's scribbling something in her notepad. "Well, it doesn't seem like the Prozac's working to control your symptoms the way it used to. We can try upping the dose. If that doesn't work, there are other SSRIs to consider."

"Mmm," I say, which is easier than the truth; a few days ago, I stopped taking the Prozac she prescribed me. Back when I was in ninth grade and my numbness was at its worst, both my neurologist and Dr. Waverly told me Prozac could help control cataplexy in people who have narcolepsy. Not because they're depressed, but because it helps regulate the sleep-wake cycle, which is what causes the muscle weakness in the first place, and even though they couldn't fully explain my symptoms, and even though they didn't think I actually had narcolepsy, they both thought the pills were worth a shot. So I tried it. And the attacks stopped, for the most part. But I guess I've always been worried there's something wrong with my brain, not just my hands or the way I sleep. That my doctors have been tricking me all this time. I don't like that thought. At all. And now that I'm talking to Jenny, I really don't like that the Prozac makes me feel less . . . sharp. Like I'm sort of soft all over.

There's nothing good about that.

"Mmm?" Dr. Waverly repeats. Like I said, she's a shrink, and I decide right then and there not to tell her about the panic attack I had in gym class. I mean, I don't want to end up in a hospital ward or something, locked in one of those rubber-walled rooms where you can't get out without a court order.

"I've got a date," I offer. "On Friday."

"A date? With whom?"

"Just some girl from school. She's in my grade. She plays the piano, and she's really pretty. Smart, too."

"The piano? So you have something in common?"

"Yeah, but I'm a pianist who can't play when my hands don't move. Plus I like jazz. Jenny's more of a classical girl."

"Are you two sexually active?" she asks.

I shift in my seat. "Uh. That's kind of a non sequitur, isn't it?"

"Is it?"

"Um, yeah. Sort of."

"I thought we were talking about what you can and can't do with your hands, Jamie."

"I thought we were talking about—oh, never mind. And nah, with Jenny, we just, you know, flirt a little and touch sometimes. Nothing serious."

"So you'd like to get to know her better?"

I stare at my feet. I don't want to feel embarrassed. Not about something like this. "Look, maybe I haven't done it yet, but I know about sex. The internet can be very . . . educational in that regard. And I know how to be safe. My real mom had me when she was eighteen. She had Cate when she was sixteen. I don't plan on repeating history, okay?"

"Okay."

I sit there. I wait for her to ask what set off my nerve attack. I wait for her to ask something, anything, so that I can bring up Cate and talk about what it means to me that she's out. That she's calling my phone. That she claims she's coming back to Danville to see *me*.

And that I'm kind of freaking out about it all.

But Dr. Waverly doesn't ask. Instead she sticks with the sex thing and runs with it, because that's what she thinks I really need. Or maybe that's what she thinks my unconscious wants to talk about.

Or whatever.

I give up, so I run with it, too.

TEN

After my therapy appointment, I hike up the canyon road to the Murphys' house. They live on Blue Ridge. My own house isn't much farther, maybe a half mile more up Oak Canyon, on a private drive at the very top. A lot of the homes around here are built on stilts. We've even had to evacuate a couple times when the rain falls for days and the mud starts to move, but nothing bad's ever come of it.

My mind tumbles with thoughts as I walk, until I feel light-headed. Cate. Scooter. Jenny. I sort of wish I'd asked Dr. Waverly if we could have spent my session today doing one of those guided imagery exercises she sometimes leads me through when I'm feeling extra tense or down on myself. Sounds lame, I know, but we used to do it a lot when

I was a kid, and I always felt more relaxed after spending time in my happy place, which is a mountain lake, in case you're wondering. I also feel bad about lying to Dr. Waverly about the Prozac, but what can you do? I don't want to take pills for the rest of my life. I took enough when I was younger, and it's not like I don't know what's making me anxious.

No one answers when I knock on the door and ring the doorbell, so I sneak around the back of the Murphys' enormous mansion. My fingers remember the gate code better than my mind does. I type the four digits and wait for the light to turn green. Then I pull hard on the wrought-iron handle and step into the yard.

Scooter's black Lab Lady bounds for me, shoves her wet nose against my crotch. I push her away. I don't like dogs.

"Hey, Scooter," I say when I find him reading in an Adirondack chair not far from his family's sport court. The rain hasn't returned, but the ground's wet and the air is, too. There's a basketball nearby, but despite his long limbs and lanky height, I doubt he's been shooting hoops. Most likely, the ball belongs to one of his stepbrothers, who are both away at college. Scooter Murphy's always been just as unathletic as I am, though I suppose a lot can change in two years.

Scooter rips his earbuds out and puts his book down. I glance at the title. It's one of those Stieg Larsson books.

"What're *you* doing here?" he snaps. "And don't call me that, by the way."

"Don't call you what?"

He gives a wave of his hand. "That kid name. My name's Scott."

"I know what your name is."

"Then use it."

The light-headedness returns, worse than before, and I almost turn and leave right then. I don't need this. His anger. His spite. All directed at *me*. Only I have to tell him. That's the thing about guilt, I've learned.

It's *compulsive*.

"Cate's out," I say.

"Shit," he says, followed by, *"Shit."* Then: "Whatever. I don't care. I'm not going to care."

"She's coming back."

This gets him to look. Scoot—Scott's face goes pale. It's a shock against his dark curls. "Coming back *here?*"

"Yes."

"You sure?"

"Sure, I'm sure. She left me a message. Listen." I hand him my phone.

He listens, then hands it back. "Why? What does that mean? What's in Danville that she could possibly want? And what the hell did *you* do to piss her off so badly?"

"I don't know. I just—I thought you should hear it from me."

"Look, man. I don't want anything to do with your crazy sister. Not after Sarah. Not ever. And I don't want anything to do with *you,* either. I thought I made that clear."

"You did. But—"

"But nothing. You picked your side. Deal with it."

"But Cate's *family!*"

Scooter glares. My words hang between us, and it's like I've betrayed him all over again. Lady puts her head in his lap. "Get the hell out of here, Jamie. And tell your sister to stay the fuck out of my life. Permanently. Let her screw yours up this time, okay?"

I leave.

ELEVEN

I've tried to put myself in Scooter's position over and over. Would I be able to forgive him if our roles in the barn fire had been reversed? If Sarah had been my girlfriend and Cate had been his sister? But it's impossible to say. I am who I am *because* I'm Cate Henry's brother. I can't help it. That's the reason the end of our friendship is as tied to Cate's actions as I like to imagine my hands are.

You know, *fate*.

It makes sense, in a morbid kind of way. Like the way they say a bird in the house means a death will follow shortly. My hands going numb that day at school with Scooter felt like a sign, an omen, like I should've known what was coming. Like I should've been able to *do* something.

Only the damage had already been done.

Mostly.

It was right after we heard about the barn fire that the cops came pounding on Angie and Malcolm's front door. They demanded to talk to Cate, who hadn't bothered to show up to school that morning. And even though I wasn't there, I can picture Angie swinging the door open wide and waving them in grandly, hurrying them up the stairs.

Like she'd just been waiting for this day to arrive.

At the same time, somewhere on the other side of town, I think a part of me knew enough to be worried. Even as I sat in the nurse's office with my head between my knees, trying not to hyperventilate while Scooter vigorously explained that no, I hadn't overdosed or huffed glue or jammed my arms up inside the vending machine. I hadn't done a thing, he shouted, and I needed *help*. Like *now*. I could be having a *stroke*. Or a *heart attack*. And oh, God, what was going on with his *Sarah*?

Even as all that happened around me, a tiny niggle of worry bored its way into my heart.

Like something fiendish.

Cate, I remember thinking. *Where are you?*

What have you done now?

Then I fell forward out of my chair and cracked my head on the ground.

The EMTs that showed up wanted to know if I'd lost consciousness before or after I hit the floor. It was important for some reason, they said, but I didn't know. I didn't care.

It's not like I could have caught myself anyway.

The rumors about Cate started almost immediately. I was in the hospital ER undergoing a CAT scan of my brain along with my first neurological exam. At the same time, in a room two floors above me, Sarah Ciorelli lay unconscious, hooked to a ventilator and close to death. From what anyone could figure out, Sarah had rushed to help after seeing the fire grow from her home across the road, and the burning barn collapsed on her while she attempted to save her own horse from the flames.

Something she hadn't been able to do.

I picture Cate handling the cops the way she handled everything. Sprawled on her bed with not enough clothes on while blowing cigarette smoke out the garden window so Angie wouldn't yell at her about the smell. Angie never yelled about Cate's lungs. Just the smell.

"Look, Miss Henry," the cops would have told her, not bothering to avert their eyes from the depth of her cleavage or the space between her thighs. "We have good reason to believe that fire was set deliberately, as a way to hurt the Ramirez family. So if you know something about that and you keep it from us, then that makes you complicit. Do you know what that means?"

"Sure I do," Cate would've snapped right back. "I'm not stupid."

"Well, you recently shared some of your thoughts about Danny Ramirez and Gwendolyn Wright online."

"Did I?"

"Yes. You wrote that Danny, and I quote, 'better not be slumming around with that Gwen bitch again.'"

"Okay."

"You also wrote that any guy you can't trust needs to watch his back. That you'd make him pay."

"Hmmm."

"Isn't Danny Ramirez your boyfriend?"

"Define 'boyfriend.'"

"Do you two spend time together? Enjoy each other's company?"

"God, that's so vague."

"It really isn't."

I picture Cate puffing away even harder and looking out the window. She had to see the crowd of neighbors gathering in the street.

Talking. Pointing. Wondering.

She had to know.

Our whole town was watching.

TWELVE

Friday evening, Jenny makes my head spin when I go to pick her up. This is due in part to her outfit, which consists primarily of vertical black and white stripes. But it's more than that. Way more. She's got her hair down, and I'm drawn in by the way her bangs land right before her eyes. It's like she has nothing to hide. I could while away days, I think, looking at Jenny, at all the parts that make her whole.

Even though she grumbles under her breath about "archaic notions of female chastity," I do the thing I'm supposed to do and go inside to meet her parents. I'm nervous, on edge, a lot of which has to do with my sister, but I haven't heard from her since Wednesday, so maybe things will be okay. Maybe this will all blow over.

Jenny's folks are decent enough, chastity notions notwithstanding. Her family only moved here last year, so I don't know a lot about them. Her dad shakes my hand and asks about school and my future and how long I've been driving. I do my best to appear normal, composed, but by the time Jenny and I say our goodbyes, I'm kind of a wreck. My worrying's got this way of reproducing inside my head, so that the few become many, and where my original concern was about making a good impression for Jenny's family, my brain takes the liberty of expanding this into All The Ways I Could Screw This Night Up. The possibilities are endless, but recurring themes seem to be general awkwardness, telling jokes that aren't funny, and stepping in dog shit.

Jenny senses my nerves, I think, because as we walk down the steps of the house to where my Jeep's parked at the curb, she takes my hand and holds on to it, like it's not even something she has to think about doing. Like in the ways that matter, she's stronger than me.

I like that.

It helps me breathe.

We end up riding the BART train into Berkeley. That's where I've found this cool art theater right near the university that's showing a series of old Alfred Hitchcock films. I know it's sort of a long way from Danville, but I don't want to take Jenny to see something dumb, like one of those fighting robot movies or that comedy with all the fart jokes. I want her to see something special. I want her to see something she'll remember.

She reads the indie newspaper on the train. It's got the schedule for the Hitchcock festival. Tonight's showing is *Spellbound,* which is the one Dali designed the dream sequences for. The one where the therapist helps the guy with amnesia avoid a murder conviction after he's framed.

"I've only ever seen *The Birds,*" she tells me.

"Then you're missing out," I say.

"You really like old movies?"

"I like good movies."

"You sound like a snob," she says, but she's laughing when she does it, so I don't mind.

I shrug. "Maybe I've just got good taste. Maybe that's why I'm with you."

Jenny doesn't answer. She keeps reading. At some point during the train ride, she leans against me and I rest my chin on her head. Her hair smells good, like fresh rain and cut grass.

We walk down College Avenue together after the film. Everything's open late for the holidays. Christmas lights are up, and the street's crowded with a mix of shoppers and university students. Jenny seemed to like *Spellbound,* even though it's not close to Hitchcock's best, and I'm feeling pretty good about the way things are going. That is, until we pass this pet store that's got a display of kittens out front, along with a sign that says they need adopting, and my skin starts to crawl.

I don't know how to describe it. It's always strange seeing a word applied to animals that has also been applied to me. In ethics class we've talked about why it's not okay to call animals slaves because it demeans human slavery, so why doesn't the same apply to adoption? I mean, you can even adopt *highways,* for God's sake. But it turns out Jenny loves cats, so of course we have to stop in front of the pet store. She puts her face right by their cage and makes *ohhh!* and *ahhh!* sounds. One of the kittens, an orange one with a red bow around its neck, yawns and stretches and puts its paw on the bar between them. Jenny turns to ask an employee, some paunchy middle-aged guy, if she can hold it.

"You really considering adopting her?" the guy asks.

Jenny glances over at me. "Well, no."

He shrugs. "Can't do it, then. If I took her out for everyone that wanted to hold her, she'd be exhausted."

"Just for a minute?" I ask. "Please?"

"You slow or something, pal? Already said I can't do it."

My muscles tense. I don't like the disappointment on Jenny's face and I definitely don't like the smugness on the employee's, but there's not much I can do to fix the situation. I wish Jenny had just lied and said she was serious about adopting the dumb cat. I mean, it's not like someone can tell if you're trustworthy or not by looking at you. But I do what I always do; I turn away from the pet store. I swallow my sense of righteousness and pride.

"Let's get ice cream," I suggest, and Jenny nods.

The ice cream shop's located two doors down, and there's a long line spilling outside and into the street. Even in December. It's a real upscale place, and the flavors they serve are ridiculous—pretentious things like lychee fruit, vintage Bordeaux, and double salted caramel, but we get to taste samples while we wait to order. I choose dark chocolate, and Jenny orders honey-lavender, which makes me smile. I don't much go for the idea of eating ice cream that tastes like flowers, but I like the idea that she does. It's sweet, you know? I take a chance, reaching for Jenny's hand as we stroll, and that's when I see Danny Ramirez, Cate's old boyfriend, sitting at an outdoor café.

He's with someone. A female.

Cate.

My stomach lurches.

It could be her. It really could—Danny's always stood by Cate, for reasons I've never understood. I can't get a good look at this girl, though. Her back's to me, so all I can make out is long black hair, and when she reaches for her drink, I see white skin, slim wrists, but it's not enough. I can't be sure. So I stand there, frozen and gaping, with my ice cream cone held up to my mouth that's hanging open like all my circuits have jammed, and in my mind, I will this girl to turn around and show her face, so I can see if she's got eyes and a chin that look like mine, only sort of hard and haunted all at once.

Turn, turn, turn, I think. *Show me.*

Then suddenly, the winter wind blows and the Christmas lights sway and the *ding-ding-ding* of the holiday bells flood my senses, and the thought of seeing my sister, here, now, after all this time, well, it stops my heart and tears at my insides. It's too much. I'm overwhelmed. I don't want to know if it's her. I don't.

I can't.

I panic. Only my hands don't go numb. In fact, I have just the opposite reaction.

"Ow!" squeaks Jenny. "Jamie, what are you—"

"This way," I say gruffly, dropping my ice cream with a disgraceful splat as I pull her right around in the opposite direction. I move on pure autopilot. Jenny stumbles on the sidewalk, but I hold her up. We march forward, like dancers on a stage, skirting a loud family that's practically taking up the whole walkway, a street performer who's singing Green Day off-key, and some scruffy-haired college student who's trying to force people into signing a petition about solar-powered trees or tax-free air or one of those nutty Berkeley things.

Once we've turned a corner, Jenny pops her hand free of mine and flexes her fingers. "What was *that* about?"

I keep walking.

"Hey!" Jenny trots alongside me. Then grabs my arm. "Come on, stop."

I'm rattled, beyond rattled, really, but now that we've put some distance between us and that girl, now that I don't have to face the possibility of seeing my sister, I'm able to do what Jenny's telling me to do; I stop and I look at her.

I feel like total shit.

"I'm sorry about your hand," I say. "*Fuck.* I'm so damn sorry."

"My hand's *fine*. Jamie, what's wrong? You look upset."

"I'm sorry," I say again, but I'm shaking, and she sees that and I can't make her unsee it. "It's just, I've got issues with, well, with anxiety, I guess. It hasn't been bad like this in a long time, though."

"Anxiety? Like panic attacks?"

I grit my teeth and let my eyes roll skyward. Well, now I'm embar-rassed more than anything. "Sort of."

"Because of your cataplexy thing?"

"Nah, I've been anxious since way before my cataplexy started. Since I was a kid. But like I said, it hasn't been a problem in a long while."

Except for last Wednesday at school. During gym. When Cate called.

"Well, I'm glad you're all right." Jenny squeezes me again, then she turns her hand over and sort of brushes her knuckles gently across my forearm. Back and forth. I suck in air. Her touch is a spark on dry tinder.

"Well, I'm glad you're so damn nice," I say.

We both stand there, not talking, just looking at each other. More than looking, what we're really doing is gazing, and we do it for so long I start to get the feeling that nothing else matters.

It's a good feeling.

Better than good.

It's one I could get lost in.

THIRTEEN

At midnight, after my date, I lie in bed feeling both exhilarated and remorseful. The exhilaration comes from realizing how much I like Jenny, but the remorse stems from not kissing her when I dropped her off at her house. I could've done it. Kissed her. I even think she wanted me to. It's just, after how I acted after seeing Danny and that girl, I wasn't sure I *deserved* it.

I writhe naked beneath my flannel sheets, feeling the feelings of all the ways in which I'd like to touch Jenny. And have her touch me back. They're like a punishment, these feelings, imprisoning me alongside the terrible way I can't stop replaying the shy, small-fingered wave

Jenny gave me as she slid out of the Jeep and said good night. A *wave*. More like a tidal wave of failure.

I writhe more.

God help me.

See, this is my worrying thing again. I mean, I'm way better than I used to be. I haven't cried for no reason or fallen down any flights of stairs recently. For the most part, I credit Dr. Waverly with my improvement. Within two years after I started seeing her, I'd completely changed. I grew a full four inches, gained twenty pounds. My lisp vanished, my hair grew back in, and people stopped asking my adoptive parents what was wrong with me. I threw myself into my schoolwork until I was my teacher's favorite, and I picked up the piano at Malcolm's encouragement: His son Graham had played, but soon I played better. In fact, I played really, really well. Concert level, even. I had *confidence*.

But as much as Dr. Waverly helped, it was Scooter, I think, who did the most. He was my first real friend.

We met near the end of fourth grade, on a day when the spring sun shone into the classroom and hummingbirds danced outside the window. Our teacher stood at the front of the room and announced that a new student would be joining us. I sat up straight at my desk. The last new kid in our grade had been *me*. I wanted to be nice to this student because I knew how it felt to have people not like you. The teacher beamed and beckoned the new boy in. He was slight like I was, with big ears, preppy clothes, and an unscuffed backpack.

"Please give a warm welcome to Scott Murphy."

"Scooter," the boy said.

"What was that?"

"Everyone calls me Scooter."

I perked up even more. The new boy had a faint hint of a lisp.

From the back of the room I lifted my hand and waved shyly at Scooter.

He saw.

He waved back.

And that was that. Malcolm and Angie were beside themselves that I'd made a friend. It killed their vision that I'd grow up to be the next Norman Bates or something. The only person who *didn't* like Scooter was Cate. She turned on him one of the very first times Scooter stayed the night with me.

He was standing in my bathroom with the mirrored medicine cabinet open.

"What are all these pills for?" he asked.

I shrugged. "I need them to go to sleep."

"Says who?"

"My doctor."

Cate flounced in then, hair pulled back. She had her riding pants and boots on, and she reeked of horse. She sat down on the edge of my bathtub. Peered at the row of orange pill bottles with a frown.

"You don't need anything, Jamie. You'll sleep fine on your own if you just try."

"But I don't want to have nightmares."

Cate shook her head, then leaned down and ran the tap. Splashed water on her face and neck. "It's too hot in here. Hot as balls."

Scooter laughed, but I blushed. I didn't like bad words.

"You have nightmares, you come to me," Cate said, her voice all echoey, with her face pointing down at the drain. "That's what you used to do, you know. Until Dr. Waverly butted in."

"Who's Dr. Waverly?" Scooter asked.

"The doctor who gives me the pills."

Scooter closed the medicine cabinet and took out his toothbrush. "You have nightmares from when you lived with your real mom?"

"I guess. Sometimes they're hard to remember."

"My dad says living like that can give you trauma and mess up your brain like when soldiers go into combat."

"Scooter," Cate said in a low voice. She sat up, but the water kept running.

"He says Richmond is basically a war zone. All those gangs. You're lucky to be alive."

"Shut up!" Cate snapped, green eyes flashing.

Scooter looked at me. "You said she did drugs and stuff, right?"

I shivered. "Yeah."

Cate got to her feet. "*What* did you just say?"

"I said 'yeah.'"

She grabbed my arm. Roughly. "What did you say about our mom?"

"Nothing. I mean Scooter knows what happened to her. That she did, you know, drugs and brought str-strange men home. And that's why she got killed."

Cate's mouth fell open. Then she punched me. Right in the face.

Scooter yelped and jumped back.

I fell to the bathroom floor and curled up, holding my bleeding nose. "What'd you do that for?"

"For being stupid!" she screamed.

"Mom!" I yelled. "Mom!"

"That's not your mom," my sister said. "That's Madison's mom. And Graham's. *Not* yours."

"Shut up! Get out of here!"

"Gladly," Cate said. But before she left, she whirled to face Scooter. His face went white with fear.

"I'm watching you," she snarled. "Remember that."

FOURTEEN

When I open my eyes the next morning, I feel deprived. Not only of sleep, but of pleasure. Cate was in my dreams, not Jenny, and this fact torments me in more ways than one. I resent my sister's ability to worm her way into my mind, but it also feels like even my subconscious doesn't think I should have nice things.

Hell, maybe it's right.

Despite my frustrations—physical, mental, otherwise—when I get up, I know what it is I need to do. I throw on clothes and use fingers to smooth my hair. Then I look around for my wallet. It's nowhere to be found. I tear my room apart, searching for the khakis I wore the night before. No luck. Mild swearing ensues, but when I walk outside in the cool December morning, my wallet's right there, lying in the dew-damp driveway, totally visible from the street.

Relieved by my own carelessness, which is a strange way to feel good, I don't bother going back inside. Instead I slide behind the wheel of the Jeep and back right out of the driveway. As usual, it feels like I've gotten away with something, and seeing as I never called my neurologist to make an appointment like I told Angie I would, I guess maybe I have. I eye my hands warily.

"Behave yourselves," I tell them.

They don't answer.

I head over to the Ramirez ranch, which sits at the bottom of Oak Canyon and happens to be the place my family's black-bottomed pool overlooks. But don't think they're beneath us in any way more than altitude; Ramón Ramirez is one of the most renowned horse trainers in all the state, maybe even the country. His reputation and wealth are the envy of Danville.

I bounce along the gravel drive getting my ass smacked with every groove and divot. Then I park the Jeep between the swollen creek bed and a patch of manzanita before heading up past the main barn, which has since been rebuilt to something far more than its former glory. I don't much like looking at it, though, so I keep my head down as I pass by.

It takes about five minutes before I find Hector in the round pen with a lip full of dip. He's working with a dun-colored filly. She trots nervously, faster and faster, throwing her head in the air as I approach, and it's like we both know I don't care for horses.

Or any animals, for that matter.

"Jamie Henry," Hector says, snapping the whip in his right hand. He's got on black jeans and a basketball jersey. "How ya doin'?"

"Not good."

"Why's that?"

"I saw your brother Danny yesterday. In Berkeley."

"Oh, yeah?"

"I think he was with Cate."

Hector doesn't respond at first. He snaps the whip again, and the filly breaks into a lope. Her hooves kick up clouds of dust.

"You think?" he asks finally.

"It was hard to tell from a distance."

"You mean you didn't go over and say hi to your own sister?"

"No."

"Why not?"

"I—I couldn't." I turn and look at the woods behind the horse ranch. The cottage where Danny used to live sits up that way. Cate practically lived there with him while they were dating, when she couldn't stand to be around our parents and they couldn't stand her, either. "He still keeps in touch with her, though, doesn't he? That's how you knew she was out?"

Hector spits in the dirt. "Maybe."

"Hector . . ."

"If it were up to me, he wouldn't have anything to do with her. But my brother doesn't think rationally when it comes to your sister. He never has. Guess Danny's not so smart for a college guy, is he?"

"He loved her. Maybe love's not a rational thing."

"She burned our barn down. She hurt that girl."

"I *know* that."

"You'd better."

I straighten up. Nod at the filly. "This your horse?"

"Yup. My dad gave her to me. Not five minutes after she was born, she walked into a split piece of wood that was sticking out of the barn. Lost vision in her right eye. They were gonna put her down, but I told my dad I wanted her. Should be able to ride her soon. She's a good girl. Real good."

"What's her name?"

"Luna."

"Whatever happened to that horse Cate used to ride? Can't remember what it was called."

"Cricket."

"That's it."

"Ask your folks."

Yeah, right.

"Danny still ride?" I ask.

"Nope. Danny goes to *school*. He's studying political science. Political science don't tell you much about raising horses, though, now does it? Or about being *rational*."

I shove my hands into the pockets of my jeans. What do I know about raising horses? "Hey, you got his number? I want to be sure about what I saw last night."

Hector shakes his head. "No way. You want to stalk your sister, Henry, do it on your own time. Leave my brother out of it. He doesn't need to worry about that girl any more than he already does."

"Fine," I say, but my cheeks feel hot. What harm could it do just to *talk* to Danny?

"Kind of strange, though, isn't it?" Hector says.

"What do you mean?"

"I mean, it's kind of strange, you going out and *happening* to end up right near where Danny goes to school. You sure your running into him was just some random, chance encounter?"

Now my cheeks burn even hotter. Yeah, I get what he's hinting at, and no, I don't believe in coincidence, but it's not like I was out there looking for Cate. Definitely not.

"Of course it was random," I tell him. "What else could it be? Berkeley's a big place."

Hector spits again. "Not that big, apparently."

FIFTEEN

I drive away from the ranch and don't look back.

My whole body feels jittery. Unhinged. I stare through the top of the windshield out at the tree-covered hills. The vast California wilderness. Sweat gathers in the small of my back, and I press down on the gas. I'm eager to get the horse ranch out my sight. My memories of it are confusing, not good. This is Cate's place.

Her realm.

It always has been.

———

From the day we moved in with the Henrys, Cate spent every moment she could down at the barn, riding. Angie loved it. Angie encouraged it. At least, at first, before things turned bad between them. It's where Angie kept her own show horse and Madison's old pony boarded.

For years Cate dedicated herself to the sport, taking lessons almost every day of the week. She graduated from walking over ground poles and cavalletti to jumping real fences in front of judges and bringing home trophies. But right from the start, I hated going down to that ranch. The horses scared me and the deerflies bit me, and it felt like Cate was taking her life into her hands every time that damn pony hurled itself into the air with her on its back. The funny thing was, as we grew older, more and more, Cate wanted me there with her, watching. I preferred to spend my time hanging out with Scooter, and once, when I was eleven or twelve, I told her so.

At that point, Cate still stood taller than me—she was leggy then, thin, sparse, and only just starting to grow the kind of curves that would eventually drive the local male population crazy, much to my brotherly irritation. "What's so great about Scooter Murphy? He's boring. He's a total loser."

"No he's not. He's my *friend*."

"You mean he plays Pathfinder with you? Is that what a friend is?"

"At least he doesn't punch me in the face!"

My sister blazed. "That was *your* fault, you know. You shouldn't be telling lies about Mom!"

They're not lies, I thought, but said nothing.

Cate softened. She took my hand. "Come on. Angie's at the store. Come with me to the barn. Please? Pretty please?"

"Oh, okay." We got our bikes and our helmets and raced down the winding country road, past miles of elm trees and estate homes and people out walking their pedigreed dogs. Chin riding mere inches over my handlebars, and with the rhythmic *tick-tick-tick* of rubber kissing macadam echoing in my ears, my mind clicked back in time to root around in our years spent in the Iron Triangle. Richmond wasn't far from here. I'd looked it up online. It was maybe thirty miles east as the crow flew, but people from Danville didn't go to places like that. Richmond was in the news all the time, for bad reasons: cast as a town on the edge, full of violence and crime and constant fear. A bridge led out of the area, across the Bay, into richer, nicer places, but only the Richmond side had a toll. Nobody had to pay to get in. Poor people had to pay to get out.

Cate and I had gotten out, of course. But we'd paid more than most.

I pedaled harder, following behind my older sister and her long black hair that flowed out from under her helmet. My legs spun and spun, as if generating their own kind of magic. And that's when they came to me: The memories, those memories of our mom flooded into my mind with dam-burst force, all of them, all at once. The sweet, sweet scent of cigarettes on her clothes. The way her hair tickled me when she wanted me to laugh. But the bad moments came, too. Those things Cate didn't want me to talk about: the drugs and the men and our mom's moods and Cate's tears and being hungry and not having the right clothes to wear when the weather turned cold.

I shivered, filled at once with both longing and rage. Maybe it'd be easier if I could only have the good memories and forget the bad. Maybe then I wouldn't feel so *awful* when I thought about my mom and the way I loved-hated her for having me and leaving me all at once.

But I couldn't forget those faint, rare wisps of half-formed memory. I just couldn't.

Not even if I wanted to.

They *defined* me.

My mind cleared as we rounded the drive into the ranch, throwing our bikes down and bolting up toward where Cate's horse was boarded. I waited outside the barn and threw rocks in the creek while Cate went in.

Five minutes later she came out with the animal on some sort of a long nylon leash. I gaped. Was she going to walk it like a dog?

"What's its name again?" I asked.

Cate sighed. "This is Cricket," she said, patting the brown horse's side. The animal snorted in return.

"Cricket, uh, looks bigger than I remember." I actually wanted to say *fatter,* but didn't know if horses were as sensitive as girls on that issue. "And wasn't she black before? And had spots?"

"That was Mr. Pebbles. God. I've had Cricket for like a *year.*"

"What happened to Mr. Pebbles?"

"Angie sold him."

"Oh."

Cate reached for my hand. "Come on. You're going to ride her. I'll teach you."

"Oh, no. No, I don't want to." I dug my heels into the ground. Felt my insides flop over.

My sister's eyes widened. "You're scared, aren't you?"

"A little, yeah. I don't like horses. You know that."

She squeezed me. "I won't let you get hurt. Don't you trust me?"

"I don't trust *me*. Or . . . or Cricket."

"Come," my sister whispered. "I'm going to teach you something secret. Something I've been practicing."

I followed Cate from the barn to the riding arena. The whole place seemed awfully empty, although an older boy I recognized walked by with a wheelbarrow and said hello to Cate. He had dark skin and even darker eyes.

"Who's that?" I asked.

Cate had a sly smile on her lips. "Danny Ramirez."

"Hector's brother?"

"Yup."

"Hector doesn't like me."

"A lot of people don't like you, Jamie."

"Shut up. That's mean. And it's not true."

"It is true. I'm being honest. People don't like you because you're scared of so many things. You do what's safe. Always. You're, like, afraid of doing anything else."

"Oh, yeah? Besides your big dumb horse, name one thing I'm scared of."

Cate turned around. I expected her to be laughing at me, teasing. Instead my sister's face was very serious. Solemn, even.

"You're afraid of yourself," she said. "Don't you know that?"

Inside the arena, Cate put Cricket on something she called a longe line, and it was like an extra-long dog leash this time. She used it to make the horse walk in a big circle. Then Cate stood in the middle of the circle, and I stood next to her. I felt sour.

"I'm *not* scared of myself," I said. "That's a stupid idea if I ever heard one."

"The thing is, you don't even know who you are. But I do," Cate said. She used her tongue to make a clicking sound, and Cricket walked faster. It was like they spoke the same language. "I remember how you used to be. When you were a little kid. You were different."

"Oh, yeah? Well, who am I, then? Tell me."

"Isn't it obvious? You're Graham Henry now. Perfect son. Perfect student. Pianist. Genius. Dead boy."

"That's *awful*," I breathed. "Don't say that."

"Get on the horse."

"Huh?"

Cate said "Whoa" and brought Cricket to a halt. "Get on her. I told you I'd show you something, right?"

"Um . . ."

"Don't be scared."

"I'm not scared," I said, even though I was.

Cate walked me over and wove her fingers together to boost me up. I wanted to show her how brave I could be, so I let her lift me into the air, sliding my leg and belly onto the sloped bare back of Cricket. Cate made the clucking sound again, and the horse moved! Right beneath me. It felt like an avalanche. So much swaying and slipping. I gasped and grabbed for something, anything, but all I got were a few strands of mane, tacky with dust.

"Stop her!" I shouted. "Please!"

"Shh," said Cate.

"Cate, *don't*. I can't—I can't *breathe*."

Then I was on the ground, on my back, looking up at the ceiling of the arena. A nest of barn swallows cooed and fluttered in the air.

"Ohhh," I said.

"Are you okay?" Cate kneeled beside me. The horse stood behind her, tail twitching.

"What happened?" I asked. My head hurt. Bad.

"You had one of your spells. The breath-holding ones."

"I did?"

She bit her lip and nodded. "You were panicking, and then you stopped breathing and slid off. Good thing Cricket wasn't going very fast. She was extra careful not to step on you."

She was? "Maybe you should call Mom."

Cate frowned. "Maybe you should get back on the horse and try again. Unless, of course, you're still scared."

"What?"

"I promised you I'd show you something, didn't I?"

So I let her put me up on the horse again. But I trembled and wanted to get off almost immediately.

"Cate!"

"She's not moving, Jamie. I promise. I'll tell you before she moves. I want you to close your eyes and relax."

Relax? That was unlikely. My heart was trying to jackhammer its way out of my chest. Plus I already felt shaky and weak from blacking out, like the kids I'd seen who played the Fainting Game at school. They did their hyperventilating and choking in secret, but I always knew what they were up to. They were the ones who showed up after recess, all whey-faced and wobbly, unable to walk straight.

Cate placed a hand on my back.

"Breathe. Nice, slow breathing. And every time you let your breath out, concentrate on letting all your muscles go loose like you're melting, like you're sinking deep, deep, deep into the horse's back. You and the horse are like one. That's right. You're doing it. Just like that. Keep doing it. Keep breathing. Keep melting and sinking. I'm going to take you somewhere inside of yourself where there's no fear. None. You're doing great. Keep breathing, keep sinking, keep going deeper and deeper and deeper . . ."

I did what she said.

I felt myself slip, slip, slipping.

And then I heard her voice again. Sharp and bright. Like a ringing bell.

"Jamie. Jamie!"

I blinked. I turned my head. I looked at Cate. Then I looked down. I was still on Cricket, but she was trotting briskly and there I was riding her with both my arms outstretched.

My heart stuttered.

"Cate!" I cried. "What's going on?"

"You're doing great. That's what's going on. No, no, don't tense up now!"

"I want to get off!"

She had the biggest grin on her face. "Yeah, fine. You were doing awesome. Whoa now, Crick. Whoa."

The second the animal stopped moving, I slid off her and leaped to the ground, where I stood gasping for breath.

"I don't want to do that again. Ever." I clutched my chest.

"What's wrong? You did good."

"Cate, I don't know *what* I did. I think there's something wrong with my brain. From the blacking out. Or something."

"Mmm. There's nothing wrong with your brain. You did perfect, okay? This was my secret. I told you I'd show you something, and I did."

I was so unsettled after the horse incident, I immediately told Dr. Waverly what had happened. About the whole time down at the barn with Cate. Every detail.

"You actually passed out?" she asked.

"Yeah, I guess. Cate said I held my breath again, but I don't remember doing that."

"This happened twice?"

"No, I didn't pass out twice. The second time—it was like the opposite. I was scared to be on the horse, but then all of a sudden I was okay. Only I can't remember doing anything to make myself feel better."

"I see," she said.

"Do you think . . . does this mean that I'm, like, crazy?"

"What does crazy mean?"

"You know, hearing voices. Seeing things."

"Do you hear voices or see things?"

"No."

"Then you must not be crazy."

"Well, why can't I remember what happened?"

Dr. Waverly clapped her hands together and sat up in her leather chair.

"You conquered a fear, Jamie," she said. "That's a wonderful thing. Taking a chance like that. Embrace your success."

"But I didn't *mean* to conquer it. I don't even know how I did it."

"Does it matter?"

I stared at her. "Doesn't it?"

"You tell me."

"I thought I just did!" God, this was getting so stupid. I got to my feet and walked over to the wooden dollhouse that she kept. A mouse family sat at the dining room table. I picked one up. Sat it on the roof of the house, then tried jamming it down the chimney. It wouldn't fit. I found a yellow Tonka truck and stuck one of the mouse dolls into the driver's seat. Then I placed the vehicle on the peaked roof of the dollhouse and gave the back bumper a little nudge. The truck and the doll went spilling onto the floor.

I smiled.

"Which doll is that?" Dr. Waverly asked.

I turned around. "Huh?"

"What doll are you playing with?"

"Dunno." I leaned over and picked it up. "It's the mom."

So that got us talking about Angie, and it got us to stop talking about Cate and the horse. I didn't stop thinking about it, though. My sister, I decided, could generate her own magic, something more powerful than mine. Something even someone like Dr. Waverly couldn't understand. That's the type of force Cate was.

For all I know, it might be the type of force Cate still is.

SIXTEEN

Later that day, it turns out Hector's wrong. I don't have to do any stalking to find my sister.

Cate finds me.

I'm driving in the Jeep with the radio on when I hear my phone—that soft, syncopated rhythm of Monk's famous "Evidence."

I glance down at the screen.

Unknown caller.

My pulse picks up. I answer.

But I already know.

"Hey, bro," she says like it's nothing, like she can just do this. "Miss me?"

"Where are you?" I ask.

"Where are *you*?"

My fingers curl tightly around the leather steering wheel. It's not her deflection that gets to me. It's her voice. Cate's voice is the same. Still husky from not enough sleep, not enough food, too many cigarettes, too many—

I take a deep breath. "Driving up Oak Canyon."

"Don't crash."

"I'll try. Are you with Danny?"

"Not anymore."

"Why not?"

"Things between us weren't meant to be. He's probably in a frat these days, don't you think? He probably has douchey friends who wear leather flip-flops and Polo cologne."

"I thought I saw you with him yesterday. On College Avenue. But that would've been too much of a coincidence, wouldn't it?"

"College Avenue, huh? That's interesting," Cate says. "I guess nothing's a coincidence. Not for you. But things got kind of heated up there last night, didn't they?"

"What do you mean?"

"'*What do you mean?*'" She mocks me with one of her crueler tones. "God, you're dense. Well, for starters, last night was the night I told Danny about what I might've done with one of his douchey flip-flop-wearing frat brothers. That kind of got the shit flying. You know how it is."

"Wait, *what*? You did that to Danny? Why?"

"Why not?"

"I don't know. I guess, it's just kind of, sort of—you know."

"Kind of, sort of what, Jamie?"

I swallow. "Nothing."

"Slutty?"

"I didn't say that."

"It's okay. I *am* slutty. You think I don't know that? I let people use me, and when they're done with their using, there's less of me and more of them."

"Stop," I say. This kind of rambling is classic Cate.

"Hey, you still got that problem with your hands?" she asks.

My head is starting to hurt. A tight throbbing pain. How does she know this? How does she know *anything*? "Yeah, I do."

"What sets it off again? Tell me."

I sigh. "Getting startled. Extreme emotional states."

"Any emotional state?"

"Pretty much."

"Mmm, what about sex, then? That's extreme, right? It'd be funny, too. Like if you were jerking it and almost there, like so close, and your hands went and died on you. Unless, of course, you've graduated to finding someone who can do that for you."

I groan. Why is it that everyone around me is obsessed with my nonexistent sex life? Isn't that my job? "I'm *not* talking about this with you."

Cate laughs, long and hard. "Right. Like there's any chance you aren't as cringingly virginal as the last time we saw each other."

My grip tightens on the phone, and that's when I do pull over and turn the engine off. I unbuckle myself and get out. My ears are filled with the screech of the Steller's jays.

"Your message said you were coming back to Danville," I whisper.

"Oh, I might," she says in her fight-flighty way.

"Why?"

"What? You don't want to see your own *sister*?" Cate's voice begins spiraling up, taking on that edge I know too well. "I'm the only goddamn family you've got, James. Me! Just me! That's it!"

"I *know*."

"THEN WHY ARE YOU MAKING ME FEEL LIKE SHIT?"

"No, no, I'm not trying—you said—"

"FUCK! FUCK! FUCK!" In the background I hear a loud crash and what sounds like glass breaking.

"What was that?" I ask. "Are you okay? Is there someone with you?"

There's more crashing. I think she's dropped the phone on the ground. Maybe she's outside somewhere, because I hear a bus go by and voices, too. They sound close. Then comes a bunch of muffled breathing and a frantic, gasping, "Jamie?"

"Yes?"

"You're still there, right?"

"I'm still here."

"Good. There are things we need to talk about. You and me. Things you need to know."

I push my hair back. I'm sweating. What the hell is going on? What does she want from *me*? I'm the one who knows *her* secrets. She wouldn't want that to come out any more than I do. I kick at the front tire of the Jeep. Then I kick it again. "Have you, you know, called Angie and Malcolm yet? I bet they'd want to see you."

"Fuck you!" she screams, one last time. "You're an asshole!"

Then she hangs up.

SEVENTEEN

The thing is, it *hurts* to watch someone you love go crazy.

Crazy isn't feeling misunderstood or laughing at the wrong times or finding meaning in music that other people don't like. Crazy isn't studying hard, chasing good grades, and earning them but still ending up in the bathroom with stomach cramps before school. And crazy isn't wondering why you should even bother getting out of bed every morning in the first place when all you're going to do is crawl back into it at the end of the day and wish feverishly that everything that happened in between could be swept away and forgotten like the drab fleeting sands of time. No, *real* crazy is about taking something good and spoiling it.

Turning it rotten.

"Aaaagh!" a fourteen-year-old Cate screamed. "How dare you!"

"Do *not* raise your voice at me, young lady." Angie stood in the second-floor hallway with her hands on her hips.

"I want them back! Now! You can't do this. You can't invade my privacy."

"This is a home, Cate. There's no such thing as privacy."

"You *bitch*."

Angie's face turned red. "If I ever spoke to my mother the way you're speaking to me, I would have been put out on the street."

"Yeah, well, I don't care about you. Or your dipshit mother. Give them back!"

"Calm down. You're hysterical."

"Give them back! They're *mine*!"

Malcolm and I both stood watching them, mouths open in shock. I thought Cate was going to hit Angie the way she'd hit me, but instead she kicked an antique table, tipping some expensive-looking vase so that it shattered on the floor. Then she collapsed to the ground in a puddle of tears.

"Come on," Malcolm whispered in my ear. "Let's go downstairs."

"Do I have to?"

"Yes, let's let them work this out." He put his arm around my shoulder and pulled me with him. He led me into the kitchen. Sat me in a chair. Pulled out his secret stash of chocolate-covered almonds he thought no one knew about.

I squirmed. Through the floorboards, I could still hear Cate crying, wailing. "What was that all about?"

"I don't know." He looked down at me. "Is it upsetting you?"

I rubbed at my stomach. "I want to see Cate."

"Not right now." He handed me some of the candy.

"They've been fighting a lot recently."

"Mother-and-daughter relationships can be complicated."

"Yeah, but Cate said Mom *stole* something from her."

Malcolm frowned. He put his arms on the counter. "I'm sure you've noticed a change in Cate's behavior over the past few months. Maybe longer."

I thought about it. What had I noticed? There had been a lot more tension in the house lately. Snapping and yelling and slamming doors. Swearing, too, and breaking rules. Most of the conflict revolved around Cate, it was true. My previously warm and happy sister was changing. Becoming angry. Unpredictable. Wild.

"Your mom's just worried that Cate might be . . . experimenting."

Experimenting? "With what?"

"Look, Jamie. I know we've talked about the danger of using drugs before. Especially given how little we know about your genetic history, right?"

I stared at the counter, cool swirls of marble, and felt queasy. Yes, we'd talked about this before and, yes, I understood the implications. My mom had probably been a drug addict. She probably came from a whole family of drug addicts and alcoholics and people with Issues. That meant Cate and I had those same horrible tendencies racing through our blood. Our own biological time bombs.

Tick tick boom.

I looked up at Malcolm. "Are you saying Mom found drugs in Cate's room?"

He bowed his head. Patted my hand gently. "Let's just let them work it out. Okay?"

Two weeks later, Cate lay panting on the floor of my room. I sat at my desk. I was listening to Mingus and reading Percy Jackson. Or trying to.

"They're sending me to that bitch doctor," she growled.

"What doctor?"

"Yours! The head shrink."

I put my book down. "You're going to see Dr. Waverly?"

"Yeah. Angie says I have to. Or I can't ride Cricket anymore."

I turned to look at her, all sprawled on the floor like some helpless sea creature.

"Are you doing drugs?" I whispered. Then I held my breath.

Cate sat straight up, like a vampire rising from a coffin. Her eyes were bloodshot and wild. "Why are you asking me that? Who said that?"

"Cate—"

"They're starting rumors about me, aren't they? They're trying to set me up. They don't want anyone to know the truth. Selfish bastards."

"Angie and Malcolm?"

"Who else?"

"Cate, I can smell stuff in your room. I can smell it right now. I'm not stupid."

She scooted toward me on her hands and knees, then grabbed my pants so that I had to face her. "Look, I smoke pot to *relax*. Otherwise I'd be a fucking paranoid mess, living here." Her nose wrinkled. "With *them*."

"They're not that bad."

"Oh, you would say that, wouldn't you?"

"What do you mean?"

Cate rolled her eyes toward the ceiling. "Like you don't know. Mr. Scared to Rock the Boat. Mr. Four Point Oh GPA. You're even worse than they are."

"Maybe seeing Dr. Waverly is a good idea. You know, if you have trouble relaxing."

"Why? So she can put me on pills like you? So I can turn into a goddamn trained seal? Arf arf arf."

What on earth? I couldn't believe her. "You just said you smoked pot to relax! How is that any different?"

She waved a hand. "It just is. You wouldn't understand."

"Well, I like Dr. Waverly. And I'm not even taking any pills anymore. I haven't in a long time. Not since—"

"Not since what?"

"Not since that day at the barn . . . when I was with you and you made me ride Cricket."

Cate sat back. Her face softened. "Seriously?"

"Seriously. She said I didn't need them anymore."

My sister didn't say anything. She just stared at me.

"Cate?"

"What?"

"Do you remember Mom? Our real mom?"

"Yes," she whispered as she reached up to run her hand through my hair. A gentle caress that made me shudder. "Do you?"

"I don't know," I said. "I mean, I have a few memories, but they're so faint, it's hard to know if they're real or if I just think they are."

"Are they good memories?"

"Yes. Mostly."

Cate's chin quivered. "Then maybe . . . then maybe that's all that matters."

"You think?"

"I don't know."

"Are your memories good?" I asked her.

Cate wiped her eyes. "Not really."

"Then don't be like her, Cate. Don't do stupid things. Don't die when you're twenty-four. *Please*."

Cate started to cry.

"Oh, Jamie," she said. "I'm trying to do the right thing. I am. But—"

"But what?"

"But it's so hard!"

EIGHTEEN

I stand next to my Jeep after Cate hangs up on me. I don't move. I'm too stunned. Our first conversation in years, and it's like nothing's changed. She's still as maddening as ever, although I suppose it's not reasonable to expect Cate would come out of being locked up any *more* sane than when she went in. I still don't know if seeing her on the streets of Berkeley was a random accident or not. Is she following me? Is that what's going on? Or did my subconscious somehow put me in a position where I'd be likely to run into my own sister? The latter's possible, I guess, but I don't really like to think like that, since it sort of cheapens the whole fate thing.

The chirrup of my phone breaks me out of my dark memories and out of my dark mood. I look down and see a text. It's from Jenny. This warms me. Hearing from her is exactly what I need right now.

We go back and forth for a bit.

Her: *Thanks for the movie. I had a great time. :)*
Me: *Me too.*
Her: *There's a party tonight. Rock City. Going?*
Me: *Wasn't planning on it. Might reconsider.*
Her: *You should definitely reconsider. I'd really like to see you
    again. <3*

I hold the phone to my chest after her last message. Everything inside of me says to play it cool, but I don't feel cool. Not when a girl I like is texting me with hearts and smilies. I was honest with Dr. Waverly about my inexperience. Not just with sex, but all of it. I mean, sure, I did some of the high school party make-out thing when I was a freshman, but sloppy rounds of Spin the Bottle don't teach anyone anything about social interaction except that old-fashioned voyeurism's alive and well.

After Cate's arrest, though, people stopped inviting me to their parties. They stopped inviting me anywhere. And not that it makes up for my loneliness or for anything, but I've sort of been okay with that. Cate changed me, too. Most people at my school knew her. Knew what she was like. So it's like we've all been tainted by her and her power. I hate that. And maybe that's part of my attraction to Jenny. Moving here so recently, she never got to know Cate.

Maybe she never will.

Not if I have anything to say about it.

When I get home, the house is empty. There's a note from Angie that says she and Malcolm have gone to a holiday fundraiser for the opera all the way out in San Francisco. Charity and the arts are a big deal to them, which I guess is what happens when you have a lot of money—giving it away becomes more important than how you got it in the first place. Though maybe that's also what happens when you lose your children. Other than altruism, I can't imagine there are a lot of places to find hope after something like that.

For my part, I'm just glad they're not home. It'll make it that much easier for me to get out for the party later if I don't have to come up with a believable excuse for why I'm not staying in on a Saturday night the way I usually do. The less pressure, the better, since I'm already a little freaked about someone starting up with me tonight. Over Cate. It's happened before, and it'll happen again. But seeing Jenny will make it worthwhile. Won't it?

I was hungry when I stepped through the door, but now a lump's formed in my throat, making it seem like it might be hard to get food down. So instead of eating, I cruise the downstairs of the empty house. I end up sitting at the Steinway in the formal living room, and I tap out the intro to Hancock's "Maiden Voyage," just to say how I'm feeling.

Pretty soon it feels good, so I keep playing. A little louder, a little freer. I have a keyboard in my room that I can practice on, but when I'm in the mood, there's nothing like filling a whole house with my music. Cate used to tease me all the time about the whole piano thing, saying I did it in order to be like Graham, but I could have said the same thing about her riding. We both spent our childhood years competing with the shadows of ghosts. But that doesn't mean I want to *be* Graham or that Malcolm only sees me as a replacement for his dead son.

At least, I don't think it does.

Sometimes I'm confused as to exactly how my adoptive dad sees me. I guess I could say he *loves* me. But I have no way of telling if it's a true fatherly love, or more of a familiar type of love, the way you can love anything you own for a long time because not having it would feel like a loss. Nobody likes loss. But nostalgia doesn't make an object any more valuable.

It's a matter of perspective, I guess.

But I'll take what I can get.

NINETEEN

After a few of those early breakdowns and tantrums, Cate's mental illness roared in like a flip had been switched. Like a runaway train. Like an animal unleashed. There was no more doubt or uncertainty or *what if?* about it. Angie spent all her time trying to smooth over the trouble Cate got into, but her efforts were the proverbial Band-Aid over the stab wound because Cate never went down for the count. Nope, she kept running around town, bleeding her madness and hate over the world like it was her sole purpose in life.

There was no reasoning with Cate back then. There was no appealing to her sense of common decency. By the time she was fifteen, she slept all day and stayed out all night. She drank. She did drugs.

She broke hearts. She broke rules. The only person Cate didn't set out to drag down into her mire of insanity and misery was me. And that was because we stopped talking. Right out of the blue. She never again invited me to the barn to watch her ride. She never came into my room to complain about school or Scooter or our parents. She didn't even bother teasing me.

I'd been dropped.

So I didn't know what she was up to with those girls. The things she was doing.

I had no idea.

I had to hear about it secondhand. From *Scooter*.

"Your sister scares me, man." Scooter and I stood side by side during eighth-grade lunch period. We were both thirteen at this point. A fence ran between Sayrebrook's middle and high schools, although they shared a common campus, so we leaned, rapt, against the chain-link fence and stared out at the older students, including Cate, who was in the tenth grade.

I picked at the flowering of acne that had sprouted along my chin. "What's so scary about her?"

"Look at her. She rules this place."

"How's that?"

"There's no *how*. She just does. Hot girls have it made in this world. And your sister's the hottest of the hot."

"I don't want to hear about how hot you think my sister is. In fact, it's the last thing I want to hear about. Ever."

"Damn, Jamie, you're tough. It's like one of your balls dropped this week or something."

I took a step backward. "Trust me, Cate doesn't have anything made. And she definitely doesn't have the one she wants."

Scooter grinned. "You're talking about me, right?"

"I am so not talking about you."

Scooter didn't follow my gaze, but I squinted back through the fence and into the afternoon sun. Through a grove of trees, on a wooden bench in the cool dappled California shade, sat Cate's longtime crush Danny Ramirez. He had his arm around his girlfriend. His petite blond girlfriend. Gwendolyn. A surge of resentment washed through me, deep as the ocean, but even I knew it was simple male jealousy. Danny was the lucky one. Damn lucky.

"Don't worry about it," Scooter said. "Like I said, Cate scares me. She's got a real temper on her."

I pulled my attention away from Danny and Gwen. Of course Cate *did* have a temper on her, but that wasn't his place to say. "And you know this how?"

"Sarah told me."

"Sarah who?"

"Ciorelli."

I made a face. Sarah? What could *she* know? Sarah Ciorelli was the most spoiled, blue-blooded, know-it-all girl in our class. And like me, Scooter *used* to go out of his way to avoid her. Until recently, that is, a behavioral shift that came roughly around the time Sarah grew boobs. Really big boobs. I didn't like Sarah, but even I had a hard time not thinking about her chest, a revelation that taught me one of the first paradoxes of attraction: How much you liked a person didn't always correlate with how much you might want them.

"Sarah doesn't know Cate," I said finally.

Scooter looked at me. "Yes she does. They ride at the same barn. A bunch of girls around here do. Sarah says Cate's like their idol, on account of how good a jumper she is. But—"

"But . . ."

His voice dropped as he leaned closer to me, one hand still on the chain-link fence. "Sarah says Cate does weird things with them, sometimes. Real crazy shit."

"Weird things?"

"Like taking them out into the woods and having them lie naked on the ground while she puts them into these trances. And if they don't listen to her and do exactly as she says, she goes insane. Like crazy mad . . . screaming. Throwing things."

Okay, well, throwing things, that did sound like Cate. But *naked trances*? That sounded like bullshit. "Come on, Scoot. You don't seriously believe that."

He nodded gravely. "It's true," he said. "Ask Sarah."

"I will."

Scooter's expression turned wistful. "God, I'd love to see Sarah ride a horse."

"An acorn fell on her head once during a meditation, and Cate totally lost it. Called us all evil little witches. Like we were the ones who made it fall." Sarah Ciorelli lay stomach down on a lounge chair by the pool in Scooter's backyard with her slim ankles crossed behind her. Scooter had gone inside to get some drinks, and I'd been left trying to coax information out of Sarah. This was no mean feat, considering one, she didn't like me very much, and two, I was having a hell of a time trying to ignore the magnetic effect her bathing suit was having on the lower half of my body. I might as well have been trying to ignore the laws of gravity or the need for oxygen.

"Why, that doesn't sound like Cate," I said, reaching up to wipe the beads of sweat running down my brow.

Sarah laughed. "Either you're more clueless than I thought or you don't know your sister very well."

"What do you mean?"

"Are you slow? I mean she's fucking crazy, babe. Like a loon. Loony tunes."

I blinked. Very quickly. "Well, what are these meditations for?"

"What are they *for*? Relaxing, I guess. Finding inner peace? Some kind of New Age crap. Who knows? I'm not your fucking therapist, Jamie. Don't make me interpret shit for you."

"Scooter said something about trances."

"Yeah, she's into hypnosis."

"Hypnosis?"

"Inductions, whatever." Sarah fiddled with her earrings so that they made a jangling sound. "She's good at it, too. I'll give her that. Said she taught herself how to do it in order to help someone she knew, only it didn't work out or she gave up or something. But she can get people to *do* things. She got Lacey Braden to quit biting her nails and she got Alicia Dahl to have her first orgasm."

I sputtered. "*Cate* did that?"

"Well, Cate says *they* did it, not her. She says all hypnosis is really self-hypnosis. It's just a matter of being suggestible."

"Oh," I said, feeling both horrified and confused because I didn't believe in hypnosis at all. It ranked right up there with street magic and faith healing in terms of things I knew I'd never be dumb enough to fall for. But also, hold up—girls had to *learn* how to have an orgasm? My world was rocked. To the goddamn core.

"Obviously, *I* never did anything like that." Sarah wriggled herself off her elbows. My eyes, with a mind of their own, made me glance down her top, embarrassing me so much that I looked away quicker than the time I walked in on Grandma Karlsson in the bathroom.

"Obviously," I said. "Tell me what else she does."

"Don't get bossy with me, Jamie. I don't like that. Use a nice tone." *"Please."*

Sarah peered at me over her Armani sunglasses. "That's better."

I stared at the ground. My stomach twisted in a way that made me feel sick, but I said nothing. I wanted to, of course.

But I didn't.

"Anyhoo," she went on. "One time she brought this hookah to pass around. My asthma was acting up so I only smoked a little, but in my head I was thinking, oh, it's just hash, you know? No big deal. Come to find out she'd put *opium* in there. Guess you can't take the ghetto out of the girl, right? Well, after everyone's wasted, Cate whips out her iPod and turns on some African drumming track. She starts dancing around, really shaking her ass, saying that something in the actual rhythm of the music is capable of altering our brain waves. We just have to *let it*. She called it a shamanic journey and said we'd all find our own personal power animal if we were ready."

I was aghast. "You're serious? She did that?"

"Yup. Some of the girls swear they saw her levitate. For just, like, a second."

Um, okay. Well, that was about the dumbest thing I'd heard yet. I turned and waved as Scooter opened the back door and came out with his arms full of Coke and Otter Pops. Then I looked back at Sarah.

"So did you?" I asked.

"Did I what?"

"Find your power animal."

"Nah, I fell asleep. Cate found hers, though. She told us."

"What was she?"

"A tigress."

TWENTY

I'm still sitting at the piano in the living room as the light starts to change, day fading to night. The timer throws on our exterior Christmas lights, and tiny white stars bounce around outside. They should be cheery, warm, full of nostalgia. Instead, a heavy sense of gloom settles in my bones the way dust and mites have settled into the folds of the velvet drapes that line the room. Twilight depresses me. It always has.

I don't bother with the tree inside. It's fake anyway.

I replay my earlier phone conversation with Cate. I should be used to her rage by now, but that doesn't mean I have to like or accept it. Other people don't act that way—totally irrational, without any thought to consequence or caution. Dr. Waverly told me once that while you can't control having an emotional *reaction* to something, it's always possible to control how you *respond*. I don't think Cate gets that, though. Or else she doesn't care.

As I get up from the piano bench and stretch my legs, it dawns on me that while I'm pretty sure Hector heard it from Danny, I still haven't figured out how my own parents knew Cate was out. They said it wasn't the courts that contacted them. So who was it? This question gnaws at me, like a dog at a bone. There are a couple of ways I could try and find out the answer, but since we've been studying Occam's razor at school, I choose the simplest.

Sneaking into Angie's second-floor office isn't a difficult thing to do. It's not like she locks the door or anything. What's hard is swallowing my sense of subversiveness. I mean, I'm not perfect, but most of the time, I go out of my way not to break rules. Why should I go looking for trouble?

Except when you do.

I ignore the voice inside my head, that little whisper of my guilt and shame, and I fire up the Mac. While waiting, I rifle through Angie's desk a little, looking to see if maybe Cate sent a Hallmark card from juvie announcing her release and everyone just forgot to share the good news with me. But there's nothing. I do find a picture of Madison, though, in a small gold frame. That's sad to look at. She was a cute girl with brown hair and a silly grin, the kind of kid you want to buy stale cookies from or teach to ride a bike. Angie was there when they died, when the train clipped the back of her minivan. But sort of like when my mom got shot in front of her two small children, the train accident is something I've never asked or wondered about. Some horrors aren't meant to be recalled.

The log-in screen appears on the monitor. It asks for a password.

I try the obvious things, like Madison and Graham and my own name and even Cate's. Nothing works. Not the name of Angie's Dutch Warmblood, Athena. Not her birthday or Malcolm's. Not the date the four of us went to the county courthouse and finalized our adoption, nearly a full year after Cate and I moved to Danville.

Then an idea comes to me. I don't like it . . . but what do I have to lose?

I take out my phone and navigate to the local news site. Here I search for Angie's name. The train crash and following lawsuit were big stories at the time, unlike my mother's death, which didn't warrant anything more than a blip on the police blotter. Rich people dying, though: That's another matter altogether. Especially when kids are involved.

I find the archived story. I look for the date of the accident.

04/12/2001

I type the eight digits into the password box.

The desktop loads.

I exhale.

Maybe some horrors aren't meant to be recalled, but it's clear Angie is nowhere close to forgetting.

TWENTY-ONE

I didn't ignore what Sarah Ciorelli told me about Cate and those girls. Not at all. After hearing about the weird things my sister had done, I'd stormed right home. I had to know if Sarah was telling the truth. Not just about the drugs and random acts of cultural appropriation. But about the way she made the girls listen to her. About her *power*.

I tore Cate's room apart. She was bad at hiding things.

Or else she didn't care if they were found.

In the bottom of her closet I found a tin of organic breath mints, rotted shut with organic mold, and a half-empty bottle of rum. Bacardi something. I unscrewed the top, smelled it, and made a face. Awful. In the back of her desk drawer she had a bag of weed and two pipes. One was metal, but the other was made of glass, all swirly with purples and blues, like a bruise that lingers. I found a second bag wedged in the drawer, too. But this one was filled with pills and a glossy piece of magazine paper folded tight with care like origami art. Inside was a yellowish-white powder.

I folded the paper right back up.

Next, I crept into her bathroom, a place I hated with its frightening contents like jumbo-sized tampons, hair removal strips, and drip-drying undergarments. Cate's medicine cabinet was lined with orange prescription containers, the way mine used to be. But instead of Valium and Ativan, she had pills with names I didn't recognize. Topamax. Seroquel. Something that was probably her birth control pills, only I couldn't verify this because I hastily put it back after seeing the words *menstrual cycle* written on the label. The rest I tried jamming into my pockets, but my hands were all slick with sweat and one of the containers slipped from my grasp. It rolled across the floor and under the linen closet.

"Crap," I muttered. I settled everything else on the floor and lay on my stomach to reach around for it. My shirt sort of pulled up so that my bare skin rubbed against the ceramic tiles, picking up dirt and stray hairs like a lint roller. Finally my fingers closed around the pills. And then something else—an envelope, a large one, was taped to the bottom of the hand-painted armoire.

I pulled them both out and sat up. The envelope was faded, lined with creases and water stains. Then my heart stopped.

It had the words *Amy Nevin* written on the front.

Our mother. *My* mother.

I fumbled with the brass clasp and shook the contents into my lap. There wasn't much. Some papers and a single faded photograph.

I inspected the papers first. The first two were photocopies of birth certificates: Cate's and mine. I'd never seen them. I smoothed them in my lap, running my fingers along my name, my stats:

James Ellis Nevin
6 lbs., 3 oz.
19.5 inches
Mother: Amy Catherine Nevin
Father: Unknown

Cate's was similar, except she was bigger, more impressive:

Catherine Grace Nevin
7 lbs., 6 oz.
20 inches

I looked at the third photocopied document.
It was a copy of our mother's death certificate:

Deceased: Amy Catherine Nevin
Date of birth: 6/22/1978
Date of death: 11/5/2002
Cause of death: blood loss due to accidental
              discharge of a firearm

I felt queasy. And hot. All at once. My mother had been *murdered*. That's what I'd always been told, so what was "accidental discharge of a firearm" doing on her death certificate? I plucked up the tiny photograph that had been in the envelope. I held it before my eyes.

A moan escaped my lips. It was a photo of two children. A girl and a boy at a park. The girl looked maybe six or seven, with twin black braids that curled out like adders and a winning smile. She was leaping in the air when the picture was snapped, back arched, hands above her head. The boy standing to her left was lesser in every way— smaller, fairer, paler. He had a blue T-shirt on and no jacket and brown cords so short his calves showed. He was scowling, and he looked miserable. Or pissed. Both, really.

I swallowed hard. Okay, *I* looked miserable and pissed. Because I knew who these children were before I even turned the photo over and saw the words handwritten on the back in the prettiest cursive I'd ever seen.

My owl and my pussycat—Catie and Jim, Thanksgiving 2001

Oh, oh, oh. I lost it then. I couldn't help it. I put my head against my knees, curled up like a pill bug, and wept. For this sorrowful scrap of fate I'd been born into. For my mom whom I'd barely known, but who might've died in some horrible way I no longer understood.

But most of all, for my sister who was doing God knows what and heading down a similar path of self-destruction.

TWENTY-TWO

Angie's email program opens right up. She has folders for personal stuff, business stuff, and her charity work. I look in the personal first, since I'm pretty sure that's the most appropriate. The charity one is tempting, but I know I'm just being a cynical dick when I think that. Adopting a child isn't charity toward the kid any more than brushing your teeth is charity toward your mouth. But it's not exactly comfortable living in a world that believes the opposite to be true. The things I've heard over the years have ranged from how lucky I am to live with the Henrys, to being asked straight-faced if it's easier knowing my mother didn't willingly give me up. To which I answered: (1) How would I know that? and (2) No.

Most of the email correspondence I find is from Malcolm and Angie's family members. This includes Grandma Karlsson. We haven't seen Grammy K in years. She stopped traveling after Grandpa Karlsson's stroke, which has been just fine by me, if you want to know the truth. Angie also has a ton of emails from her friend Penny Parker, whom I hate. Penny's loud and rude, and worst of all, she's not half as funny as she thinks she is. She always insists on comparing me to her son Dane every time she comes over. It's like a 4-H competition that I'm destined to lose. This is because Dane, who's two years older than me, is perfect. He's currently a freshman at a nearby college where he plays lacrosse, has a hot-ass girlfriend, and never deals with things like idiopathic cataplexy or anxiety or a psychotic drugged-out horse-murdering sister blah blah blah, you get the picture. Dane's doing fine on his own, so I'm not sure what the point of making me feel awful about myself is. But there was some trouble between Cate and Dane a while back, which is why Penny does the comparison thing—to make herself feel better. Whatever. For all you hear adults talk about how insecure and attention-seeking teenagers are, I think they're the ones with the real issues.

Among the emails from Penny complaining about her tennis game and her divorce settlement and whether or not Dane's girl comes from a good enough family, I don't see anything from my sister. I quickly browse through her other folders, but there's nothing in those, either. The only folder I haven't looked in is the trash. I click on the icon. Sort the messages and search for . . .

I inhale quickly.

There they are.

Three messages all from wildcatnevin24@gmail.com with receipt dates from the past three weeks.

All have the same subject line:

the owl and the goddamn pussycat

I look at the oldest email first.

My chest burns.

It's about *me*.

TWENTY-THREE

That day more than three years ago when I sat in Cate's bathroom, gripping the photo of myself as a child, was the first day I truly understood the depths of Cate's illness. Her instability. Her bleak, lost future. But when you're thirteen *understanding* isn't the same thing as *empathy* or *compassion* or *a call to action* or any of those words that might actually be helpful. Back then, understanding was just a thing that made me scared. I'd lost my mom, and now I was losing Cate. Who would I lose next?

Then a noise came from outside—a car door slamming shut in the driveway like a gunshot—and I jumped to my feet. I couldn't let anyone find me in here. I tore from the bathroom to the front-facing window of

Cate's bedroom and looked down to see her wrapped in Danny Ramirez's arms. The art of contrast: He was dressed in dark jeans, hand-tooled cowboy boots, a wide-brimmed hat, while she wore fishnets and a black dress hiked up so high her garters showed. Cate leaned against Danny, hip bone to hip bone. She ran fingers down his cheek, his neck, his chest, a light territorial tracing, then said something to him. He laughed and pulled back. Tipped his hat to her.

Got into his truck and drove off.

I sprinted back to Cate's bathroom and gathered up everything I could, the papers, the pills. I couldn't hold on to the rum bottle, so I thrust that under her linen closet with my foot, then bolted for my own room, slamming the door shut behind me. I threw her things into my closet, then flipped on my keyboard and slid headphones over my ears. Heart jammering, I ran my fingers across the keys, forcing out some scales and chord progressions before settling into Brubeck's frenetic "Take Five." It was the fastest song I could think of. I focused on the rhythm, foot tapping wildly against the hardwood floor.

Someone touched my shoulder.

"Gah!" Nerves quintupled, I leaped about five feet into the air before whirling around. There stood Cate, cheeks flushed with some inner heat and both hands placed firmly on her hips. Long rips ran up and down her stockings, but I knew she wore them that way on purpose.

I pulled the headphones off. We stared at each other. I couldn't remember the last time she'd come into my room voluntarily.

"How's Danny?" I asked lamely.

Her expression turned smug, like a cat standing over a bowl of milk that'd been poured for someone else. "He's good. Very good, in fact."

"Isn't he, uh, going out with Gwen?"

She shrugged. "We'll see who he asks to the Winter Formal next month."

"You know, I th-think Dane might like you."

She snorted. "I think Dane might get his dick cut off one of these days if he doesn't watch where he's trying to stick it."

"Oh!" I said, alarmed, although there was a tiny part of me, deep inside, that wouldn't have minded all that much if she'd actually gone through with that threat.

"So what are you up to?" Cate asked.

"Nothing."

"Nothing?"

More silence. Cate eyed me like the tigress she claimed to be, green eyes glittering and sharp. Like the turning blade of a knife.

"How did Mom die?" I blurted out.

Her eyes narrowed. "Why're you asking me that?"

"Well, they never caught the guys who killed her, right? Maybe—"

"Maybe what, Jamie?"

"Do you think she could have, uh, could she have, you know, killed herself?"

Then all of Cate's edges melted. She ran over and hugged me for the first time in months, all softness and warmth and a sort of ripe, sweaty odor that reminded me of old socks and made me think maybe she wasn't that clean.

"God, *no*. She would never have done that. Never. She loved us. She didn't want to die. Trust me."

I felt like crying again, but didn't want to do that in front of Cate. "Did she . . . did she ever used to call me Jim?"

"Do you remember her calling you Jim?"

"Yes," I lied. "I think I do. I think I remember that."

A faraway look came over Cate. Like sorrow and satisfaction all at once. She kissed my forehead hard enough for her lipstick to brand my skin.

"Hey," I said, leaning out of her grasp. "What was that for?"

She smiled her wide Cheshire grin, the one I'd never understood and never would. "For being you."

TWENTY-FOUR

I take a shower before I go out. The hot water and soap feel good on my bare skin, lather and needly pinpricks slicing off the layers of dust and sweat that I've collected.

It's been a long day.

Too long.

I try to forget about Cate and those creepy emails and whatever the hell's wrong inside her head. The things she'd written to Angie were rambling and vaguely threatening and mostly incoherent. I didn't understand any of it. I didn't even understand the connection to "The Owl and the Pussycat" poem, which was something I'd looked up after finding the title of it written on the back of a photo our mother had taken. But it had all been nonsense.

Like Cate's emails:

(you can't pretend i don't exist angie)
(jamie's the one i want he was mine before he was yours and he'll be mine again)
(the past is what matters angie you've been brainwashed if you think otherwise)
(you can't hide him from himself not anymore)
(i'm coming for him)
(i'll show you)
(i'll show everyone)
(bitch)

Part of me is sad for my sister and part of me is angry. Angry that she's been set free into the world without any help for her weaknesses, for her sick, sick mind. Angry that Angie hasn't done more to reach out to her. Cate's her daughter, after all, no matter how she's disgraced herself and our family. A mother's love should be stronger.

But I'm also angry that Cate wants something to do with *me*.

My stomach burns, nearly doubling me over.

Why didn't anyone tell me about Cate getting out sooner?

Why didn't someone *warn* me?

The voice inside my head returns.

You know why, it says.

Because you deserve this.

I feel sick. I stumble from the shower and grab for the jar of Rolaids I keep on the edge of my sink. My insides have a way of getting bad when

I'm stressed, which is another one of my body's depressing reminders of how constitutionally frail I am. It's like my stomach gets filled with acid or I swallow too much spit. I chew a chalky handful of the antacids, then drink a glass of water. Then another.

When I can breathe again without pain, I stand up straight. I close the cabinet door and wipe away the condensation that's gathered there. I've managed to grow a little stubble across my upper lip and along my neck, so I'll have to shave if I want to look halfway decent when I show up at the party tonight. I pick up my razor and look at myself in the mirror.

What the *hell*?

I peer closer. I run a hand across my own face. Most of me looks normal, like what I am or what I've become: your average suburban white kid, one with brown hair and blue eyes, and who is remarkably unremarkable. I've had people tell me my lips are my best feature, which is meant to be flattering but always makes me cringe. Some guys can pull that off, having more feminine features, but suffice it to say I am not one of them. But that's not what I'm looking at right now. No, it's my *eyebrows*.

Patches of hair are missing from my eyebrows.

A sliver of fear scrabbles up my spine.

I've been pulling at them again. That's pretty obvious.

Only I can't remember doing it.

TWENTY-FIVE

I drive myself to the party. Rock City's not close, but it is secluded, which is what matters. A steep cluster of stone caves line the western wall of Mount Diablo, north of Danville, and the whole area is hidden from the main road. During the summer, the state allows overnight camping, but only teenagers with nowhere else to go come up here during the other three seasons. For good reason. Ten years back some kid got drunk and fell while crawling out of one of the caves in the rain, pitching over the cliff and smashing onto the rocks below. Rumor has it his ghost still hangs around, waiting to shove other kids to their plunging death. But if you ask me, the most shocking thing about the tragedy is that it hasn't happened again. Trust me, there's usually a whole lot of stupid going on up here.

Dread and anticipation war inside my chest.

On the side of good, there's Jenny.

On the other, there's my sister.

My fears about someone starting up with me about Cate are not unfounded. I've had to deal with it for years now. It's not about having a criminal for a sister; it's about what happens when your sister makes a lot of people very unhappy.

Sarah wasn't the only one who spread rumors about Cate. Even before the fire, Hector Ramirez had something against her. He let me know about it not long after Sarah blabbed to me about the things Cate was up to in the woods near the Ramirez ranch.

The day Hector approached me, I was sitting in a library carrel reading Richard Wright's *Black Boy* during lunch. I'd felt unwell of late, since finding that photograph and the information about my mom's death. But who could I talk to about it? Talking about it meant admitting I'd stolen the items from Cate, and the guilt from that made me feel so bad I couldn't stand it. So instead I sat in the library, straining to absorb Wright's hunger for food, for life, for *everything*.

"Tell your tramp sister to leave my brother alone," Hector muttered under his breath as he passed by.

I dropped the book and whipped around in my wooden chair. "*What* did you just say?"

He paused. "Your sister. She's all up on Danny these days. It needs to stop."

"That's between her and Danny."

"No, it's between me and you now. Danny's going places. He's going to be *valedictorian*. He doesn't need to be dragged down by girls like that."

"What do you mean, 'girls like that?'"

Hector's eyes lit up. "Manipulative. Lying. A complete and utter bitch. Do I need to go on? I've heard about her, you know. What she lets guys do to her, and what she'll do for them. She comes from trash. She's trash. Put her on a leash, man."

Rage crackled in my mind, and flames danced in my line of vision. I shoved my chair back and got to my feet. "Don't you *ever* talk about my sister that way."

Something in my expression made Hector take a step back. "Why? What're you going to do about it?'"

"How 'bout this." I shoved him in the chest with both hands. Hard.

"Yo, Jamie, don't do that! No, really. Don't." Scooter leaped from nowhere to come between us. He dragged me back. "C'mon, he's not worth it."

"He's talking about *Cate*. He called her a tramp!"

"That's his problem."

"He called my mom trash, too. My *mom*!" My voice sort of cracked, but Scooter kept pulling me away, toward the nearest exit. He talked to me the whole time, his voice low and rational and soothing.

"Don't worry about it, Jamie. Cate can take care of herself. Hell, she'll probably take care of him, too. You know her. That girl's got balls of steel, man. She wouldn't want you to do this."

"But—"

"But nothing. Just calm down. Jeez, you're like, shaking."

We stepped outside. I wrenched free from Scooter and leaned against the metal railing of the wheelchair ramp. The sky was hazy, like my mind, and it was hard for me to breathe. I didn't understand what had happened. I wasn't a fighter. Far from it. I had the heart of a pacifist. The mind of a coward.

My hands tingled from where I'd put them on Hector's chest, and I couldn't get his biting words out of my mind. I closed my eyes. I hated feeling this upset, and I hated that Cate had put me in a position where I felt I had to defend her honor. I especially hated that her honor was something she didn't even bother to value in the first place.

That was what really upset me.

More than anything.

TWENTY-SIX

I leave Dr. No parked in a tight spot, wedged off-road, between trees, and head over to the party. Too Short's blasting from a set of speakers mounted in the bed of an F-150, and there's a long line of white kids snaking around a pony keg. This is pretty much the definition of irony, if I've ever seen it, but seeing as I'd take Monk over Macklemore any day, who the hell am I to talk? I'm as full of shit as the next guy. I just keep my head down and avoid the whole scene. Everywhere, all around me, the night air smells sharp, raw, like eucalyptus and mud.

I end up hiking around for a while, trudging past picnic tables and campfires, but I find Jenny at last. She's sitting on a stone ledge with a group of her girlfriends from school. I recognize them, her friends.

They're quiet girls, not the pretty or popular ones, but the ones you can tell read a lot and think deeply about things. Too deeply, maybe. The girl equivalent of me, I guess is what I'm trying to say.

Jenny looks up as I get closer. She grins when she sees me, and the moment this happens, everything else slips away. I'm drawn in like a moth to the world's most benevolent flame.

"Hey," I say, coming to a stop so that I'm standing directly in front of her. I let the toe of my shoe touch hers.

"Hey," Jenny says right back, tucking a piece of hair behind one ear. The girls she's with giggle at the sight of me and hustle off into darkness as if on cue. Nearby, a bunch of senior guys are already crawling past a large sign that reads DANGER: DO NOT CLIMB. THERE IS GREAT RISK OF DEATH OR BODILY HARM and lowering themselves into the caves.

I sit beside Jenny on the ledge, inching as close as I can.

"You look nice," I say, which is lame, but at least it's something. That's an observation I've made over the years: When you're quiet, saying something is almost always better than saying nothing. There's less chance of being misunderstood that way.

"Thanks, Jamie. You look nice, too."

"I do?"

She nods, but then points to my eyebrows. "What happened here?"

"Oh. Nothing. Just a bad habit."

"You pull them?"

"Yeah. I've even been known to get the lashes when I'm really stressed."

"So you're anxious *and* stressed?"

"Sort of," I say, and well, crap. Now I'm wishing I'd kept my dumb mouth shut. I grit my teeth and brace myself for the inevitable next question.

Why?

But it doesn't come. Instead Jenny sways backward, almost tipping off the wall before catching herself and laughing. I pull her upright.

She laughs even harder. That's when I realize she's drunk. She slides a thin clear bottle from her jacket pocket and shoves it at me. I read the label. Peppermint schnapps.

"Where'd you get it?" I ask.

"Greta's brother. He's home from Santa Cruz this weekend. She stole it from his room. Have some. It tastes like Christmas."

I take the bottle but don't drink any. "I have to drive."

"Oh, just have a little. Otherwise I'll feel stupid. Like you'll think I'm just some dumb drunk girl."

"No I won't," I say quickly, but the worst thing is that that *is* a little bit how I feel. So I listen to Jenny and swallow a few sips of the schnapps. It's sweet and spicy and burns all at once, but soon I'm warmer, looser, and the awkwardness between us fades. Jenny curls against my chest, and it feels natural to put my arm around her. To hold her. She's a small girl, and her bones have this avian lightness to them, like grace. Like truth.

Like everything good.

"Jenny bird," I say, without meaning to, and Jenny crawls closer in response. All the way into my lap.

I hold my breath at the weight of her, at how damn good it feels to have her on top of me. Both my arms are wrapped around her now. I don't want this moment to end. I won't let it.

She turns her head and looks up at me. Her lips part.

I lean close to hear her words.

Jenny says, "Tell me why your sister set that fire."

TWENTY-SEVEN

I exhale.

"My sister has issues," I say.

"It sounds like it."

"Who told you about her?"

"No one told me anything. But when that guy in the hall brought her up the other day, I went online and read about what happened. It's *awful*. Did she really burn that barn down and kill all those horses?"

"Yeah. She did."

"But *why*?"

"I don't know," I say. The warm buzz in my head is fading. I need water. I feel parched. Wrung out. "Supposedly she was pissed at her boyfriend for hanging out with some other girl. An ex. I don't know if that's true or not, but he's always stood by Cate, so maybe it is. And she's never said anything more about it. I don't think she ever will."

"Well, what happened to that girl? The one who was in there?"

I shake my head. "Her family moved to Texas. She was being treated at a burn center there, last I heard. It was pretty bad. Not just the burns, but a head injury. The trauma."

"But your sister, she was messed up before that, right? I read she used to manipulate other girls. Get them to do, you know, *things*. And that she trashed some guy's sports car."

"Mmm," I say. "There was never any proof about the car. And those girls did what they did with Cate willingly. It's not like she put a gun to their heads or something."

Her nose wrinkles. "But still. People called her a *witch*."

"It's just gossip, Jenny. I'm not saying she's a saint, far from it. But don't believe everything you hear about Cate."

"Well, I had no idea. I mean, it must have been terrible for you. A terrible time."

I shrug. Of course it was terrible. It's not like something like that can have an upside.

Jenny presses her cheek against my shoulder. "I wanted to ask you about it last night, when we were in Berkeley. But you were already sort of upset. And—"

I bristle. And what? And now she's drunk and doesn't care about upsetting me?

But Jenny runs her fingers along the line of my chin, very gently, thawing me a little. "And I wanted you to have a good time. I didn't want you to be sad."

"I *was* having a good time. It's just . . ." Right then it's on the tip of my tongue to tell her. About how almost maybe running into Cate is what set off my panic attack last night. About the weird phone calls and messages. About those emails I read.

But I can't get the words to form.

"It's hard to talk about," I say, at last.

"Are you going to see her now that she's out of jail?"

"I don't know."

"Do you want to see her?"

I shake my head. "I don't know what I want. That's the truth. I don't know."

"Well, it's okay not to know, right?"

"Is it? That's something else I don't know. I don't know if it's okay not to know!"

"Hey!" Jenny says sharply. "Stop that."

I blink. "Stop what?"

"This." Jenny reaches up and pulls my hand from my brow. I'm stunned. I'm pulling hairs again.

Without even realizing it.

I writhe away from Jenny, sliding her onto the ledge beside me. Then I sit facing forward. I hang my head in my hands and stare at my shoes in the dirt. My feet are huge compared to Jenny's. Monstrous even.

"You're stressed about your sister," Jenny offers.

I nod.

Jenny rubs my neck. My heart thumps in its dramatic-erratic kind of way, and I can feel myself getting worked up. That's not a bad thing, but the thought that's rattling around inside me, twisting my gut and stirring up dread, is that I don't want my hands to go.

Please don't let my hands go.

"I know I can't exactly understand," she says. "But I do know what it's like to have someone you love get locked up. I've got a brother, Tobin, he's twenty, and he's had issues since he was a kid—acting out, having rages, unable to control himself. He saw all kinds of doctors, got all sorts of diagnoses, but we had to put him in a residential home when he was seventeen, on account of my parents couldn't control him anymore when he got mad. He even hit my mom once, gave her a black eye and a concussion. He felt bad about it later, but still. We didn't know what else to do."

"Shit, I'm sorry, Jenny. I didn't know that. That's really sad."

"Yeah, it is. It's really fucking sad. At least your sister got out. My Tobin'll be in there forever."

Cate wouldn't be out yet if it weren't for me, is what I want to say. *She shouldn't be out. She's dangerous in all her witchy ways,* and maybe confession is what my soul needs. Maybe then I'd feel less weighed down by sorrow and by shame. But I don't say those things. I don't say anything because Jenny keeps rubbing my neck, and her hand's creeping down my shirt, toward my chest, and even lower. I sit very still while she does this, but then she's laughing again and her breath reeks of booze, so I turn around.

"I should get you home."

Jenny makes dreamy eyes at me. Either she's half asleep or she wants me to kiss her. I should probably know the difference, but the sad truth is, I don't.

"You okay?" I ask.

She nods. Then shakes her head.

"I don't feel so good."

"You want to go?"

"Yeah," she says. Then: "I can't walk."

"I'll help you."

Jenny huddles in the passenger seat. She's shivering something awful, so I put the heat on high. Then I put my jacket over hers. I don't have a blanket or anything.

"Tell me if you're going to get sick, all right?"

She smiles at me. "I'm just cold. And tired."

I nod, putting the Jeep in reverse and backing up. "Good thing we're getting out of here anyway. These things never end well. Look at that."

Jenny's gaze follows where I'm pointing. In the icy night air, juniors Nicky Johnson and Matt Calvin are squaring off in a drainage ditch, throwing punches at each other. Both have their shirts off, and it's like they think making a spectacle out of beating up someone else will give them power. I guess they don't know it's the crowd cheering them on that has the power, not them. A bunch of varsity athletes, including that asshole Dane Parker, who must be in town visiting his mom, are all standing around with their phones held up, recording the whole thing.

"Remind me not to drink again, okay?" she says.

"I sure will."

"I feel embarrassed."

"Don't."

"You're so nice, Jamie. Greta says you've always been shy on account of your sister, but you don't seem shy to me."

"What do I seem like?"

She snuggles close, leaching my warmth. I put an arm around her as we start to drive down the mountain.

"You seem good, Jamie. Real good. You make me feel safe."

TWENTY-EIGHT

Of course Jenny does get sick on the ride back to Danville, somewhere near the base of the mountain before we get back to town. I pull over and help her. I hold her hair. She cries a little bit, which makes me sad, but I can't make her feel better. She has to learn her limits the hard way. I don't hold it against her. It's how I learned, after all.

The first time I drank, I was fourteen and Scooter stole a bottle of Jose Cuervo from one of his dad's pool parties. We mixed it up with red Gatorade and took turns doing shots in his bedroom while watching *Iron Man*. At some point during the night we decided it would be a good idea to wrap Scooter in aluminum foil and crash a Sayrebrook party down the street. The only thing I remember is walking into a house packed wall to wall with people I didn't know, and getting separated from Scooter. Next thing I knew, I was lying in my own bed with the morning light trying to burn holes through whatever brain cells I had left, and Cate was standing over me with a funny smirk on her lips.

"You are so busted," she told me.

I groaned and pulled the covers over my head. "Go away. I feel awful."

"How much did you drink last night?"

"I don't remember."

"Yeah, well, Angie's *pissed*. Nice going. Now you can deal with her shit instead of me."

I peeked out from under the blanket. The sunlight hit my eyes like daggers. "Angie knows?"

"Yup."

"How?"

"Mmm, I think the fact that someone puked red stuff all over the entryway when they got home last night might've tipped her off. And by someone, I mean you."

"*I* did that? Are you serious?" The thought made me want to puke red stuff right then and there. All over my bed. "Oh, God."

"Completely serious. Like I said, nice going. I'm probably supposed to give you a lecture on the dangers of underage drinking, but why bother? She's going to *kill* you. That rug's an heirloom, by the way."

"I'm dead. So dead." I flopped back. "And what happened to you last night?"

"What do you mean? I was at the Young Equestrian awards ceremony with Angie. I was on my best behavior, too. Snoozefest, but whatever. I got a new dress out of it. Shoes, too."

I shook my head, then quickly regretted the motion. "No. I saw you. Last night. I could've sworn I did, at a party down on Donegal Way."

"Wasn't me," she said.

"Yes it was."

"You're wrong."

We stared at each other.

"So how're things going with Dr. Waverly?" I asked weakly.

"Things are going swell, Jamie, love. Really, really swell."

"She's helping you?"

"Hmm. I don't know if I'm supposed to say that. It's not empowering, right? I'm supposed to say that I'm helping myself. That's the correct way to phrase it, isn't it?"

I swallowed. She was right. That was exactly what Dr. Waverly would say.

"Did she end up giving you any medication?" I asked, thinking about the pills I'd found in her bathroom. I'd looked them up online. They were for treating *bipolar disorder*. And *psychosis*.

"What would I need medication for?"

"For whatever you're, uh, seeing her for."

"I'm seeing her because of Angie's insecurity that I won't turn out like her perfect little Madison. That I might want to be my own person someday. That I might want *you* to be your own person, too."

"Oh," I said.

Cate stared at me. "What kind of medication do you think I should be taking for all that?"

I shook my head. I didn't say anything.

"What're you reading there?" She pointed to a magazine lying beside my bed. "Graduated to *Playboy* yet?"

I squirmed. "It's *The Believer*."

"Don't tell me you've found religion."

"It's a literary magazine."

"A what?"

"Never mind."

She frowned. "You know what your problem is?"

"What?"

"You care about things that don't even matter. Like, you really, really care. But none of it matters. Nothing you know means anything, Jamie. Remember that."

The weight of her gaze was too much. I looked away.

"So wh-what's up with you and those girls from the barn?" I stammered.

"What girls? What do you mean?"

"I just heard that you've been doing things. In the woods."

"Doing *things*?"

"You know, teaching your, uh, friends, how to do . . . stuff. And other stuff."

Something dark came over her. "Who told you this?"

"I don't know."

"Was it that stick-up-her-ass Sarah?"

I said nothing, but a bloom of dread was already working its way through my veins. I didn't have to answer or nod or admit anything. Cate could read my mind. Always.

She swept her hair into a ponytail with a huff. "I gotta get down to the barn. Dressage this morning."

"You really weren't at the party?"

"I really wasn't. Now sleep it off. I think you're still drunk. And Jamie—"

"Yeah?"

She headed for the door. "Let this hangover be a lesson to you. You're too fucking young to be this stupid."

I collapsed with a wince. All the muscles in my body felt stiff and sore like I'd been run over by a truck. I closed my eyes and slept for another six hours. When I finally got up and hobbled downstairs, I didn't get the expected Angie lecture on "being a responsible member of this household." I didn't get anything. That's because Angie was on the phone trying to calm down Penny Parker. Penny was hysterical because someone had slashed the tires on Dane's precious Porsche Boxster overnight and pried the hood open to pour sand into the engine. Later there was talk, of course, that Cate had done it. But no one could ever prove that she hadn't been exactly where she said she was that night.

Least of all, me.

TWENTY-NINE

Once I get her back in the car, Jenny goes to sleep. It's a true sleep, she's not unconscious or anything. I keep driving, staying under the speed limit, with both hands firmly on the wheel. I feel totally sober but getting pulled over would not be good. To say the least.

Of course, I remember the way to Jenny's house because I was only there last night. But when I turn into her court and roll to a stop at the curb, I don't shake her awake or sit her up. Instead I throw on the brake and sit behind the wheel with the engine idling and the heat still going. The porch light is on and her parents seemed nice, but also kind of strict and most likely disapproving of any or all peppermint schnapps consumption, and I guess it comes down to the fact that I can't just leave her here to get busted. That protective male urge. I mull it over. I could take her back to my place. She'd be safe there with me. Angie and Malcolm would never hear us come in, and if they did hassle me, well, I'm sort of pissed at them right now anyway.

For once in my life, I'm in the mood to break rules.

A real sea change.

I twist the wheel and turn the Jeep around. I'm a quarter mile from home when my phone rings.

I pull off the road *before* I answer this time.

It's after midnight.

I *know*.

THIRTY

"Jamie," Cate says in a sort of a whine. "I miss you, little brother."

"Where *are* you?" This feels like an automated response by now.

"I'm close. Really close."

"Where are you staying?"

"Wherever I can."

"Well, don't burn any barns down, okay?" Oh, God. I'm feeling sort of crazy when I say this. I don't know why I say this.

"What? What was that? Did you say something about *barns*?"

My neck goes stiff. "Nope. No way. I said, uh, don't forget to stay warm."

"You said *barn*."

"No I didn't."

"That's not funny."

I opt for a subject change. "Cate, I saw the emails you sent Angie. I saw them on her computer. She didn't tell me you were getting out."

There's silence.

"Hello?" I say.

Nothing.

Damn it.

"Cate?"

"I'm too angry to talk right now, Jamie. I think you said something mean about me."

"I didn't!"

"I'm still angry."

"Don't be, Cate. I want to help you. I want to understand. Everything."

"I don't believe you. You don't care about me. You never wrote while I was gone. You never visited."

"You told us not to visit! You wouldn't let us! And I did write. At first."

"Not enough."

"Well, you never wrote back."

"That shouldn't have stopped you."

"Whatever," I say, because although she's right, it's not like I was having such a great time, either.

"Hey, Jamie?" she asks softly.

"What?"

"Do you remember that time Angie stole something out of my room? I'm not talking about you finding that photo of us as kids— yeah, I knew about that. I mean earlier. When I broke her vase. That handblown glass one."

I lean my head back against the seat. "Yeah, I remember."

"Do you know what she took from me?"

"Um . . . drugs?"

"*No*, dickhead. Well, that wasn't the only thing. She stole pictures of our mom! I had pictures of our real mom."

I freeze.

My hands go.

"Jamie?"

I manage to keep the phone gripped between my ear and my shoulder, but my head spins and my lungs burn, like they're conspiring against me.

"Why didn't I know that?" I squeak. "Why haven't I seen them? Cate, it's our *mom*. You know I don't remember her."

"You haven't seen them because I didn't have them anymore. Angie took them from me after I told her I was going to bring your old memories back, and that once I did maybe you'd stop loving her."

"*What?* Why would you tell her that? Shit, Cate, my hands! I can't *feel* them."

"I *told* her that because she didn't listen to me! Every time I missed our mom or wanted to talk about our past Angie wouldn't let me. She'd yell or ignore me, or worse, she'd cry. I felt bad at first, but you can only feel bad for so long when someone else's pain is hurting you, too. After a while it kind of pisses you off."

I make a mewling sound. What Cate did to Angie, what she said to her, God, it's so *mean*.

My sister's voice drops to a whisper. "Angie sent me the photos after I emailed her. She apologized, but she also told me not to come home. She's scared I'm going to ruin you next. And you know what? Maybe she should be."

"Ruin me *how*? I want to see those pictures!"

"Meet me tomorrow then. But don't tell anyone. You have to promise."

"Where?" I say. "When?"

"Crap. Someone's here. I gotta go."

"Cate, wait! Don't—"

"Later, kid."

Click.

The phone slips from my ear, and my stomach starts to cramp. I try to hold it back, but I know I'm going to puke. Like, right now. Only I can't open the car door. My goddamn *hands*. I make a frantic jab at Jenny with my shoulder, to see if I can wake her up, but then I have to use my elbow and body weight to roll down the driver's side window. Half strangled by the seat belt, I stick my head out just in time to throw up onto the street. Loudly. Then I throw up some more, and it's terrible. This is way worse than the Gatorade-tequila time because I don't think I'm going to forget this.

I know I won't forget.

This is awful,

awful,

awful.

Finally I bring my head back inside. But with my hands dead, I can't move any more than that. I'm stuck behind the steering wheel of a car I can't drive. I am utterly helpless.

Beyond helpless.

I'm hopeless.

Damn.

I close my eyes.

Cate has pictures of our mom.

Angie stole them from her.

To keep *me* from seeing them.

None of this makes sense.

My sister is crazy.

Totally crazy.

This is all my fault.

"FUCK!" Twisting with all my might, I slam my left shoulder against the door as hard as I can. The Jeep rocks, and bright stars of pain ricochet back up to my skull. I groan and rear back to do it again.

"Jamie?" a voice says, halting me mid-flail.

My heart flutters. *Oh, Jenny.*

"Jamie, are you okay?"

No, I'm not, I think. I am not okay. But as usual, I can't *say* it.

"Did you get sick, too?" she asks.

"Uh, yeah. I got really sick."

"Poor Jamie."

I grunt.

"Wait, where are we?"

I open my eyes and look over at Jenny. She's blinking and sitting up. She's still got my jacket wrapped around her, and I want her so bad that a little part of me wishes I were dead. A little part of me wishes my life weren't like this. Terrible.

But just like clockwork, the voice inside my head whispers, *You reap what you sow, don't you, Jamie?*

"My hands are messed up," I tell Jenny, because I don't know what else to do. "You want to come over to my place for the night? I was heading there so that you wouldn't get in trouble with your folks. But now, I sort of need your help."

Jenny smiles drowsily. "Sure."

"I hope you don't mind walking the rest of the way," I say.

Jenny texts her parents that she's staying with Greta.

Half an hour later we lie face-to-face in my bed. Jenny's got my sweats on, and she even helped me get my jeans off and my teeth brushed. She's falling asleep while holding on to my hands and rubbing them, and even though I can't *feel* it, just seeing her touch me is turning me on. I watch her. I watch her because she's so pretty and sweet and watching her keeps my mind off Cate.

She keeps touching my hands.

My heart keeps aching for things I can't have.

Like a clear conscience.

Like inner peace.

"Tell me again," she whispers.

"Tell you what?"

"Tell me that name you called me. Back up on the mountain."

I say it in her ear. "You're my Jenny bird."

STRAIGHT,
NO CHASER

THIRTY-ONE

Okay, here's the thing about what my sister did. I didn't know about any of it. I swear—at least, not *before* the Ramirez barn burned and Scooter's poor luckless Sarah Ciorelli ended up in the hospital burn unit, fighting for her life.

But *after*, well, I found out some things about Cate on my own. Bad things. And maybe when I found those things out, I should have handled it differently. All right, I know I should have.

Only I didn't.

And I have to live with that.

It happened like this:

In the immediate aftermath of the fire, the only thing I thought about was my hands. Oh, maybe part of me thought fleetingly about Scooter and his Sarah, wondering why she might've been dumb enough to be in a burning barn at night. But having to wait in the ER all those hours, worrying whether I'd had a stroke or a spinal injury or if some fast-growing tumor was pressing down on my cranial nerves, I mostly thought about myself.

In the end I learned nothing. My hands came back to life on their own after hours of being poked, prodded, and referred for further testing. I was discharged and sent home. Relieved, Malcolm and I drove back to the house on Oak Canyon only to discover Angie alone, and Cate long gone. She'd bolted from the house right after the police had questioned her that morning.

"She's with that Ramirez boy," Angie hissed at Malcolm the moment we walked through the front door. She didn't even look at me or the knot on my forehead from where I'd fallen down in the school nurse's office.

"I'll call over there," Malcolm said wearily. Then he patted my shoulder. "Go get some rest, Jamie. Your hands are doing all right now?"

"Yeah, they're totally fine."

"Maybe you should take a break from piano for a few days. It could be carpal tunnel or something."

"The doctor didn't think it was."

Malcolm snorted. "ER docs don't know anything. They're just there to keep you from dying. I'm going to make you an appointment with my neurologist, okay?"

"Yeah, sure," I muttered. I went to walk upstairs. Malcolm had already had surgery twice for carpal tunnel, so it made sense that that's where his mind went. But not doing things like playing piano was an overreaction. I hadn't been playing when my hands went numb. I'd just been sitting there, listening to everyone freak out about Sarah. Maybe I should stop listening to other people. Maybe that was the answer to all my problems.

"Hey, Jamie," Malcolm called out, forcing me to turn around.

"What?"

"You notice anything different about Cate recently?"

"Different how?"

"I don't know," he said, frowning.

"Yeah, well, me neither."

It wasn't long before Scooter called, hysterical.

"They won't let me see her, man! Me!"

"What? Why not?" I asked. I squeezed the phone between my shoulder and ear and lay on my back on the floor of my room. I held my hands up and wiggled each of my fingers, one after the other.

Just to be sure.

What had made them freeze up on me like that?

Would it happen again?

"I don't know," Scooter squeaked. "The hospital says it's policy. Only *family* can see her."

"Oh," I said. "Well, maybe that's true. The policy. That sounds right."

"That sounds like *bullshit*! She'd want to see me. I know she would!"

"Calm down."

"I am not calm. I am anything but calm right now."

"Scooter . . ."

"There's something else going on, too," he said. "My dad said the *cops* want to talk to me."

"Wait, what for?"

"I don't know what for. Something about the fire. They think it was set on purpose. It started in Bailey's stall, I guess, and . . ."

I frowned. Bailey was Sarah's horse. I'd heard Cate mention her before. Listening to Scooter talk, my worries about my hands began to fade. They were replaced with a heaviness in my gut, a brooding sense of dread.

"I bet it's not a big deal, Scoot," I said weakly. "You're going out with Sarah, and she was hurt. I'm sure it's standard to talk with you."

"I didn't do anything," he said in a low voice.

"I didn't say you did."

"What if she dies? What am I going to do?"

"I don't know, Scoot. Don't worry about that now. She's going to be fine. Everything will be fine."

His voice cracked. "I love her, man. That might sound crazy, but I *do*."

I sighed. Honestly, it did sound crazy. It wasn't nice, but a part of me was hoping this might get them to finally break up. It was time. I mean, they weren't exactly Romeo and Juliet. Or hell, maybe they were—two oversexed kids with nothing in common except their belief that novelty was enough to keep them together.

"Everything will be fine," I repeated.

"Have you talked to Cate?"

"No," I said. "Why?"

Scooter made a gasping sound. Sort of a laugh-sob. "It's just, sometimes I wonder about her. Remember that stuff Sarah told us? What she'd do in the woods with those girls? And we both know what the guys say about her. Supposedly there's a video—"

I stiffened. "You're talking about my sister."

"I *know*. But I've heard other stuff, too. Like how she was the one who fucked up Dane's Boxster last spring. And I know how pissed she was when Sarah's horse kicked hers during that show. Plus she's with Danny, and it's his family's barn. People are saying she was mad at him. Something about Gwen. Look, other people are talking, too. So maybe—"

"Maybe what?"

"You know."

My tone grew stern. "We are not having this conversation, Scooter. We are never having this conversation. So back off. Now."

"But this is about Sarah," he whined.

"Cate is my sister. End of story. Got it?"

He hung up.

Scooter's suspicions stewed in my mind after our phone call, and stirred me into action. I had to find my sister. I had to make sure she was okay and let her know what people were saying about her.

I also had to make sure the rumors were *wrong*.

I jumped off my bed and grabbed a jacket. I'd told Malcolm I didn't know where Cate was. Technically, this was true. But I thought I *might* know.

Without a word to my parents, I slipped down the back staircase and into the garage to grab my bike. Helmet firmly on head, I pedaled down the hill toward the Ramirez property. My lips moved the whole way. I was praying out loud for my hands to stay strong.

And for my sister to stay good.

Autumn wind and dying sun. I smelled the fire before I saw it. Nearing the ranch, I spotted rows of police cars and ladder trucks crowding the drive. The burned barn wasn't visible through the trees, but my eyes and throat stung from the smoke. I thought of Sarah and charred horseflesh and started to gag. I threw my bike to the ground and kicked it into the bushes.

Pulling my shirt up over my mouth and nose, I traveled the rest of the way on foot, scrambling up the hillside and doing my best to stay upwind from the smell. I hiked through brush and forest, slipping on dry leaves and fallen branches, until I reached the main house on the Ramirez ranch, which sat in a copse of pine trees, far from where the horses were boarded.

Hector was the one who answered when I rang the doorbell. It figured. We stared at each other for a good long time, the air crackling with ego and the simmering threat of violence. I hadn't forgotten what he'd said to me that day in the library. Clearly, he hadn't forgotten my response.

"Where is she?" I said finally.

"How should I know?"

"Because she's with your brother."

Hector narrowed his eyes. Despite his or my wishes otherwise, Cate and Danny Ramirez had been seeing each other for a while now. In a serious sort of way. It was supposed to be a secret, but like most small-town secrets, everyone knew about it. Even Danny's ex, Gwen, who'd sworn she'd get him back.

"Check in the guesthouse," Hector said. "That's where Danny stays these days."

The way he said the last two words made me wonder if the living arrangement was somehow Cate's doing, but it's not like I could just ask.

"Thanks," I said. "I'm sorry about the fire."

He lifted his chin. "Did you set it?"

"N-no."

"Then don't be sorry."

"Yeah, fine, whatever." I turned to go.

"Heard you had some kind of medical thing going on today."

I looked over my shoulder and nodded. "Yeah, I did. Something happened to my hands."

"Your *hands*? What about this?" Hector pointed to the spot on his temple that correlated to the location of my cut.

I reached up to feel the bandage. "Oh, that. Yeah, I fell or passed out or something in the nurse's office. I'm okay now, though."

"You sure? No offense, but you look kind of fucked up."

"Sure, I'm sure. Uh, thanks again, Hector. I'll go find Cate now."

"All right then. You go do that."

"Pretty sad about Sarah Ciorelli, huh?"

"There's a lot of sad in this world," Hector said, before swinging the door shut.

No one answered at the guest cottage. Set back in the woods, the small outbuilding looked like it'd been updated recently, with a new redwood deck off the side that had a view of the valley. If I twisted my

head and looked straight up, I could make out my own house perched
on the canyon's edge, mostly bright glare and sun bouncing off glass.
I walked around to the back of the cottage. An abalone shell ashtray
sitting on the deck railing with a crumpled pack of Camel Lights beside it, told me Cate had been here recently. A wind catcher woven
with feathers and sticks twirled from the eaves.

I peered through a pair of French doors but couldn't make out anything but an unmade bed and a pair of jeans. I stepped back quickly.
I didn't want to think of my sister on that bed, all sprawled and wild
and bewitching, doing whatever it was she and Danny most likely did.
Sex and Cate were topics I never wanted to think of together, no matter what rumors I heard or how much she liked to flaunt her body. I
mean, of course, I saw the way guys looked at her.

I just really, really hated it.

A low snarl escaped my throat. I leaped from the porch to the
ground, then wished I hadn't. My head hurt more. A gust of wind
whispered up the valley floor, bringing some of the sick fire scent with
it, and that's when it came to me. A faint tinkling. I turned in the direction of the noise, but saw nothing.

Then it came again. The soft tinkling of a bell. Like a lost melody.

I listened more.

It was coming from the woods.

I squeezed my hands into fists, then let them go. I'd been doing
that a lot, wanting to make sure my body hadn't betrayed me again.

I headed into the woods, winding higher and higher up the hillside. The trees closed around me, stealing the sun, leaving me shivering. I kept walking.

Maybe an eighth of a mile in, I found the source of the noise. It was a
second wind catcher, hung high off a draping oak branch. This one was
also made of sticks and feathers, but someone had tied to it a long strand
of copper bells weathered white-green with verdigris. Nudged and jos-
tled by the wind, the bells filled the air with their chaotic harmony.

Where was I? I turned around and around. I stood in a secluded hollow, deep in the woods on what must be the far edge of the vast Ramirez property.

I was washed with the strangest sense of déjà vu. Had I been here before?

Above my head, the wind catcher swayed and tinkled more. Dead leaves spun across the dirt path, making sounds like falling rain. My gaze moved from the singing bells to the massive oak branch they dangled from. The trunk of the tree was split, straight down the middle, so that half of it bent one way over a damp creek bed. The other half bent the opposite way, straight into another tree. This left a gaping hole in the center of the trunk. A deep, black hole.

I walked over. I peered inside.

Darkness.

I felt dizzy, a swirling wave of vertigo. I thought of secrets stuffed into drawers and beneath linen closets, the way squirrels store nuts—as a means of survival. My chest tightened, and I balled my hands into fists again. To make sure my nerves were still working.

Then I stuck one of those hands down inside the broken tree trunk.

At first I felt nothing of interest: a rush of cold air, cobwebs, something lumpy that might have been mushrooms. I stretched farther, plunging as far as I could go, until my armpit was hooked against the sharp bark. That's when I felt it. The tips of my fingers brushed against some kind of man-made object, also lumpy but with parts made of Velcro and nylon. I jumped and wriggled onto my tiptoes, straining and reaching even more to grasp it. Then I pulled hard, giving one huge heave. My momentum popped me free with great force, and I flew back, landing sprawled on the ground with a grunt.

But I had the object. I looked at it. And I gasped.

It was a bag, a messenger bag, black nylon with red stripes. And I recognized it because it was *mine*. It'd disappeared from my room last year and I thought maybe Angie had thrown it out, but now I knew who'd taken it.

Cate.

I shivered as the wind whipped through the clearing, bringing up goose bumps on my bare arms. There was a part of me that didn't want to be here. That part was telling me to get up and leave.

Go, a voice inside my head said. *Don't do this. Don't. Some truths aren't meant to be known. You love your sister, no matter how screwed up she is. She's all you have. Don't let anything change that.*

But like a soon-dead cat, my curiosity got the better of me.

So I sat up.

And I opened the bag.

The process of dumping the items onto the ground and sifting through them was one of desperation. I wanted what I would never find: proof of my sister's innocence. Proof that she wasn't as bad as everyone made her out to be.

Proof that her magic was real and I wasn't destined to lose her.

But instead, kneeling in dust and pine needles on a bright October afternoon, I found that the contents of the bag included:

- Three books on the subject of hypnosis.
- One bottle of cheap gin (I knew it was cheap because it came in a plastic bottle and had a $9.99 orange clearance sticker from Big Lots! on it).
- One red-lined notebook in which Cate had recorded all of her induction experiments with the girls and the wicked things she'd made them do.
- One pair of thick fire-retardant gloves that reeked to high heaven of gasoline.
- One silver butane torch lighter.
- One disposable cell phone with a history of text messages that had been sent to Sarah Ciorelli's number between 12:43 and 12:47 A.M. the night before.

Hands shaking, I scrolled through the individual texts. Each was more agonizing to read than the one that had come before it.

Together they added up to a crime far worse than arson:

hey sarah.
look out your window
hope you're not slow
better be fast
better hurry
better
run.

What I did next is hard to explain. It's also hard to live with.

Believe me.

Earlier that day, mere hours after the fire, an anonymous caller had told the Danville police all about the bag hidden in the woods and where to find it. But it wasn't until the next morning that the cops actually went looking for it. By the time they made their way into the forest to arrive at the broken oak tree beneath the feathery wind catcher, the messenger bag and all its incriminating contents were gone.

Vanished.

Forever.

Buried in a place I'll never tell.

In the somber weeks that followed, Cate was the lone suspect, but without evidence, no arrest was made. The tension in Danville grew unbearable. Picturing Cate dousing Danny's family's barn in gasoline as payback for his perceived infidelity didn't take a huge stretch of anyone's imagination. Not only did she have a motive, but she was well-known for her moods. Her irrationality.

Her fiery temper.

Still there was nothing to be done from a legal standpoint. A dark stalemate formed between Cate and the world around her.

Then these things happened:

Scooter moped and stopped talking to me.

Sarah regained consciousness, but remained in intensive care.

Angie fretted and began seeing her own therapist again. Twice a week.

Malcolm suffered in stoic silence the way he always did.

My hands kept going numb. The doctors freaked, and I convinced myself I was slowly dying.

And so it went for weeks.

Until the day I stopped going to school. Not because of my hands, but because the guilt over what I'd done made my stomach burn so badly I couldn't leave my room. I was in agony. Dr. Waverly came to the house to see me, and I overheard her talking with Malcolm about admitting me into an inpatient treatment program for panic disorder. That was the first time in my life that I thought seriously about killing myself. With a rope. In my closet. This was also the day that Cate marched downtown to the police station in the bright autumn warmth and confessed to setting the barn on fire in a fit of misguided rage.

Judgment was swift: On the eve of my fifteenth birthday, my sister was sentenced to thirty months in a juvenile detention facility for arson. I was in my room the morning she came to say goodbye. She didn't mention the conversation we'd had the night before as I huddled hamsterlike on the end of her bed. Cate simply drifted into my room looking pale and tired and walked straight to my bookcase where she plucked my copy of *Black Boy* right off the shelf. I watched as she ran her finger across the title.

With her back still to me, she asked, "What's that quote you like so much in this book? I heard you telling Malcolm about it. The guy goes to vote, and he writes something on the ballot."

"He writes, 'I Protest This Fraud.'"

Cate turned around. Her eyes were full of tears.

"Oh, Jamie," she said. "Don't let anyone else tell you who you are. Ever."

"Okay," I said.

She bit her lip. "I . . . I did a bad thing once."

"I know."

"And I don't know how to make it better."

"You can't," I said.

She handed me the book.

"I want to try."

3

PLAYED TWICE

THIRTY-TWO

On Sunday morning, Angie does that thing she always does. She knocks on my door with the backs of her knuckles, tap-tap-tap, then opens it before I can answer.

"We're leaving for church in ten minutes," she says brightly. Then she freezes.

I sit up, chest bare, hair all rumpled, my mind swirling with memories of Cate and what she'd done and what I'd done and how I'd do anything to get my hands on a photo of my real mom.

Anything.

My hands.

I look down. My hands are working again.

Then I realize what Angie's looking at.

It's not me.

It's Jenny. Beautiful Jenny who's curled beside me, eyes shut tight, soft blond hair spilled across my pillow like a promise. She's so beautiful that seeing her fills me with a twinge of melancholy. Like she's too good for me or I'm not good enough for her, both of which are true, I suppose.

I glance up at Angie.

"Shh!" I say in a tone dark enough to startle us both. "She's sleeping."

Angie frowns, lines forming on her otherwise perfect face, but she retreats and closes the door. Okay, she slams it.

Beside me, Jenny stirs and smiles as her eyes flutter open.

"Your mom's going to hate me, isn't she?"

"I won't let anyone hate you," I say.

Jenny stretches, arching her back in a way that enchants me. "How very chivalrous."

"Is that so bad? Chivalry?"

"It's only bad if the sole romantic gesture you have to offer is saving me."

I'm not sure what Jenny means by this, but she's smiling when she says it, which reassures me I haven't done anything wrong.

"Your hands are all better," she says.

"Yeah, they are."

Jenny reaches out and rubs my fingers, like she did last night. Only I can feel it this time.

It still turns me on.

"Jenny," I say hoarsely.

"Yeah?"

"I really like you. That's not chivalry talking, either. I swear."

"I like you, too," she says, and then she kisses me.

Jenny kisses me.

I lean back, and I let her. It's transcendent, this kiss, this skin on skin, this her touching me touching her. After a while, I reach up to wrap my arms around her waist, and we keep kissing and touching until we're both breathing hard. Until waves of pleasure are pulsing through my body like sizzling streaks of fireworks rocketing through the new year's sky. Until there's nothing more I want than to be with her like this, right here, right now. For a long, long time. Forever, really.

I want to lose myself in this moment.

I want to forget

the empty ache where my mother should be,

my sister's madness,

my own rotten feelings of guilt,

my complicity.

I want to forget it all.

But even in this most perfect of perfect moments,

I can't.

THIRTY-THREE

The fooling around thing Jenny and I are doing is interrupted by my phone.

No, no, no. No way. Come on.

I try ignoring it. I try focusing on my mouth and breath and skin against hers, this moment I've felt only in my dreams.

It's touch.

It's taste.

It's so much more.

But . . . Monk.

I groan. I pull back and pick up my phone.

Unknown caller.

"I have to answer this," I tell Jenny. I roll out of bed and walk across the oval hooked rug to stand by the window. Outside there's a hint of sun, and a pair of sparrows flit around the branches of the Japanese maple in the side yard. "Cate?"

"Hey, boner."

My fingers grip more tightly around the cell phone. There's a certain level of apprehension that comes with talking to someone you know is capable of murder. Especially when they don't know you know. "This isn't the, uh, best time."

"No? Why not? What're you doing? Are you *fucking*?"

"What?" How does Cate do this? "No!"

She yawns. "You sound horny."

"My God, Cate. What is *wrong* with you?"

"Wouldn't you like to know?"

"Yes! I would!"

I hear her smoking. Picture red-stained lips on gold filter. "Nah, never mind. Look, are we on for today or what?"

"Just tell me when and where."

"Jesus, you want me to do, like, everything."

"Cate, I don't know where you *are*."

She laughs, a strange, uncontrolled giggle. "Me neither. I'm way too high right now. It's, like, you're asking me metaphysical questions."

"I'm asking where you want to meet! I want to see these pictures you have. The ones of . . . Mom."

There's a long silence. I fret. Have I pissed her off again? I'm pulling at my eyebrows, and I am fully aware of it. This is too much. She is too much.

"Peet's on Highview at one," she says finally.

"Peet's?"

"Or else."

Click.

THIRTY-FOUR

It's 1:33 P.M.

My sister is late.

She's late, and I'm sitting in a corner of the coffee shop by myself with a cup of way-too-strong coffee that insists on burning a hole in my stomach no matter how much milk and sugar I put in it.

It's not like I should be surprised. Growing up, Cate was known for her lateness. To everything and everywhere. School. Church. My recitals. Christmas dinner. Her own surprise party that *she* planned for her sweet sixteen. It used to make me so mad, like she got some sort of sadistic pleasure out of making people wait. Dr. Waverly tried to tell me people sometimes did stuff like that when they felt they weren't in control of other aspects of their lives, but even with all of Cate's issues, I never bought into that.

Crazy or not, control's sort of her thing.

I snatch a newspaper off the empty table beside me and try to read. It's local and predictably dull. Last night was the holiday light parade, and today there's a candle-making workshop downtown. Oh, and the farmer's market has extended hours all the way up until Christmas Eve. Such events are Big Deals around here, because we're Rich People pretending to have Small Town Values. However, there's also an editorial expressing concern that "those" type of people are prowling around Danville again. For emphasis, this article includes a picture of a homeless family who's been staying in their Honda Civic at a nearby park. The caption beneath the photo reads: THEY CHOOSE TO LIVE THIS WAY, and well now, that is some nice holiday spirit going on right there, let me tell you. Jesus.

Below the fold, I also learn there's been a spate of home robberies over the past few days. Mostly cash and prescription meds have been stolen, along with some jewelry, and despite the not-even-trying-to-be-subtle implication that the unfortunate Civic family might be involved, it's like the bottom drops out of my gut when I read that.

Over the past few days.

I set my coffee and paper down.

I'm giving her ten more minutes.

That's it.

Right then Scooter walks in. He's preppy as hell in his khakis and Sperrys. He's also got this *fuck-it-all* swagger to his walk that I've never noticed before. Not that I've been looking or anything, of course, since up until last week, I've pretty much ducked my head and avoided Scooter Murphy at all costs for the past two years. Today, however, he's with a crowd of Sayrebrook students, including a couple of girls, and I realize I don't know if he's hooked up with anyone at all since Sarah. For his sake, I hope so. No, it's not a nice thought, considering, but trust me, she wasn't any kind of a catch to begin with. She wormed her way between us. Acted like she was better than me because of where I came from. That's not the sign of a kind person, making others feel bad about who they are and what they have.

The group bunches up at the counter, ordering things like gingerbread lattes and peppermint mochas with whipped cream. They all have pink noses and pink cheeks from the cold. For all I know they're coming in from an afternoon of sweaty group sex, but at the moment they look so damn *wholesome*. All that's needed is snow falling outside and Christmas carolers and an open fire or sleigh or whatever it is that that song says. I look away, feeling a sharp tightness in my chest and that hollow pang of loneliness. I have an urge to text Jenny, but it's been all of an hour since I dropped her off. I don't want to seem needy.

I think I am needy.

"Henry," Scooter calls out.

I look at him, startled.

"What the hell happened to your Jeep?"

My cheeks burn. Gross, I know, but I didn't have a chance to wash it before I drove down here.

"I don't know," I say.

"Looks like you blew chunks all over it."

"I guess it does."

"Must've been some party." Scooter wanders over toward my table. This makes me wary for a number of reasons. One, I doubt his sincerity, and two, I can only imagine the sparks that might fly if Cate strolls up while he's standing here.

"It was okay," I say.

"Sounds more than okay. I heard you left with Jenny Lacouture. She's cute, man. Real cute."

I don't answer. Jenny's *mine*. Jenny's not gossip.

"Guess some girls really do go for that loser virgin thing, huh?" Scooter leans into my personal space to run his gaze over the newspaper in front of me. He's scanning the article about the robberies.

"What's this?" he asks.

"Nothing."

"You sure?"

"Sure, I'm sure."

He smirks. "Sounds a lot like—"

Cate walks in.

I look at her.

She looks at me. Then she looks at Scooter.

She turns and runs.

"Cate!" I yell, and Scooter laughs in my face. He doesn't see her. I jump up, managing to bump the table and spill my coffee. The cup flips onto the floor, and the lid pops off. I push him out of the way.

I run after my sister.

THIRTY-FIVE

"Cate!" I call again when I get outside. To my left, I catch a flash of her jeans and the olive-green hoodie she's wearing. She's sprinting down the sidewalk at top speed. Her legs move like racing pinwheels, and I run as fast as I can. My heart's pounding and my fingers are tingling, but my hands still work.

For now.

Cate doglegs it down a narrow alley that leads to the parking lot behind the store. Barely breaking stride, she reaches down and snags a loose brick out of a sagging planter box. As she passes behind my Jeep, she rears back and heaves the brick through the back window.

The glass shatters. The alarm begins to blare.

"What the hell are you doing?" I screech. I fumble for my keys. I want to turn the alarm off before the cops get called. Hell, in this neighborhood, they'll probably get called anyway.

Cate stops dead. She stands there, staring at the broken window, like she can't believe what she did, either. In the hand that didn't throw the brick, she's got this pink bag, she's holding on to some stupid shiny pink bag.

I run right up to her. "Hey!"

She spins to face me.

I gasp.

Her face. Even after all this time and all this heartache, Cate's face is the same as it always was—beautiful and clear and sculpted in all the right ways. She's black hair and high cheekbones. She's green, green eyes and red, red lips.

She's just so *miserable.*

"Cate," I say, and I already know it's going to happen.

I just know it.

"You set me up!" she screams.

My hands go.

The keys fall to the ground.

I try to breathe. I try to keep breathing.

"That's my *car*!" I choke-squeak. "You threw a brick into my car!"

"I know!"

"*How* did you know it was mine? How could you know that? Have you been watching me?"

Cate's nostrils flare but she says nothing. Nothing from Cate means yes. It means guilt. And I'm gut-rot sick of her guilt.

"Look what you did!" I holler, and I'm talking about my hands and my Jeep and *everything.* "I did not set you up!"

Cate balls her fists and screams. It's an awful sound. Full of pain and insanity.

My knees shake. My sister is a force I can't control. "Look, I want to know what's going on. I read those emails you sent to Angie. You keep talking about *me*. Like I did something wrong!"

She claws at her throat. She leaves red lines in her own flesh. "You're trying to hurt me, Jamie. You always hurt me. That's what's wrong."

"How am I hurting you? I ran into Scooter *by accident*. All I want are those pictures. Please. I have a right to see them!"

Cate's face goes pale. For an instant, I think she's going to turn and bolt again. Flee my life in her hit-and-run way. But she doesn't. She takes a deliberate step toward me.

Then another.

"What did you say?" she asks.

"N-nothing."

"You think you have a right to everything, don't you? You always have."

A right to *what*? God. I take a step back.

My head is swimming.

My heart feels like it's slowing down.

"I don't feel so good," I say.

"No way," she growls. "We're not doing this bullshit. You need to listen to me. For once."

I don't know what bullshit she's talking about. I don't care, either. Colored dots burst before my eyes.

"Cate, I can't, I can't *breathe*."

My sister grabs for my dead hands and yanks me toward her. "Stop it, you little coward. Do you hear me? Don't you *dare*—"

Everything goes black.

THIRTY-SIX

When I open my eyes, I'm bleeding. I taste blood. I taste hot copper.

My senses return slowly. I hear voices. I feel pain. I realize I'm lying on the ground in the parking lot behind Peet's. My left shoulder is half submerged in a greasy puddle, and a whole group of people I don't know are crowded around me, their eyes wide with curiosity and concern.

Cate is not one of them.

"Don't get up," some guy in skinny jeans says.

I groan. "What happened?"

"We think you passed out," a dark-haired woman tells me. "We found you here."

"Your lip's bleeding," a second woman says. She's standing beside the first, and she's wearing a gray hooded sweatshirt that reads I'M THE DOULA. "Your forehead is, too. Not bad or anything. But still."

I lift my arms. Move my fingers. My hands are working again. That's good, at least.

"I think I'm okay."

"Should I call an ambulance?" the guy asks. "You look real pale, kid."

"No," I say. I'm always pale. I roll over and manage to get up to one knee. I grab for my Jeep keys, and my head teeters wildly. Did I really pass out? That's more than a little humiliating. Maybe I'm more hungover than I thought. I press my fingers to my hairline. It feels sticky, but I don't think my brain is leaking out or anything.

What's wrong with me?

Where the *hell* is Cate?

I look back at the three strangers. "Did any of you see a girl here? She's got black hair. About my height?"

"We didn't see anybody. Just you," says Skinny Jeans. "You sure you don't want me to call an ambulance?"

I shake my head. I'm Magic-8-Ball cloudy. Cate *was* here, right? It's sort of hard for me to remember. "N-no, thanks."

The guy eyes the car keys in my hand while the two women gape at the shattered rear window of the Jeep. The dried puke on the driver's side door.

The doula looks back at me.

"I don't think you should be driving," she says slowly.

"I'm fine. I really am." I smile and attempt to appear normal, not deranged or drug-crazed or whatever it is they're thinking about me. I sidle toward the Jeep and try not to panic when Skinny Jeans pulls out his phone and starts dialing. That's when I jump in, slam the door, and start the engine.

As I peel out and drive off, I don't look back.

———

Twenty minutes later, I'm at home. I've also locked myself in the bathroom.

I'm in a state of mild hysteria, a feeling akin to waking up with my hair full of water bugs or being forced to walk blindfolded across a long stretch of thin ice. Not helping matters is the fact that I'm pretty sure Angie's on the phone with Malcolm right at this moment. This makes me feel shitty, like I'm a shitty person, because I know he's probably at the golf course, trying to spend his Sunday alone, the way he always does, and now his tranquility's being ruined with the news of how I came home with a bleeding head wound, a broken back window, and no memory of how I got hurt.

My lungs make a frantic wheezing sound. I put the lid down on the toilet and sit there.

I can't catch my breath.

My chest hurts. Everything hurts.

What the fuck just happened?

Goddamn Cate.

I start shaking then. The vibrations originate deep inside me, a sick and fallow rumbling, like something volcanic.

I kick out with my left foot, tipping over the stainless steel trash bin and scattering tissues and cotton balls all over the floor.

But it's not enough.

I reach out and sweep one arm across the glass shelf above the sink. Toothpaste and toothbrush and dental floss and razor go flying.

Still not enough.

I stand halfway and press harder on the shelf, leaning more and more with my body weight until it snaps and shatters, glass falling on porcelain. Falling everywhere.

Still.

It's not enough.

I am only beginning to erupt.

My breath comes in sharp bursts. I bend over to pick up the chrome scale Angie bought for me when she was worried the Prozac might make me fat, and with a yelp, I hurl it straight at the medicine cabinet. The mirror explodes in a giant crash, sending shards of glass shooting back at me, peppering my neck and hands, before hailing down onto the floor.

For a moment I don't move.

At all.

I simply stand there, in the middle of the bathroom, blinking and shell-shocked.

Then I drop to the ground. I quickly grab the trash can and a towel and start sweeping up the awful mess I've made. My knees crunch on glass, my hands bleed and sting, but I don't stop. I work faster. Frantic and frenetically. I need to get rid of this before anyone can see what I've done. *I* don't even want to see what I've done. Getting mad, losing control like this, it's not like me.

It's like *her*.

Once I've got all the glass cleaned up, and I've washed my hands and lined all the non-broken toiletry items neatly on the edge of the tub, I use my shirt to wipe at my brow and sit back on my haunches. My foot brushes against something. I turn and look.

And groan.

It's Cate's pink bag. The shiny one. I'd found it sitting on the passenger seat of my Jeep where she must have left it before abandoning me unconscious in a public parking lot for strangers to find. I mean, who *does* that? I could've been dead for all she knew. I snatch the bag up with a snarl. Part of me wants to toss it away and be done with my sister. Be done with all of this for good. But I don't.

I open the bag and reach inside.

My fingers touch tissue paper, all crumpled and thin, and because hope and anger can't coexist, my ire melts away. I'm seeking images of my dead mother. I need them. I need her. I'm owed that much, aren't I? The only thing of hers I've ever touched, besides Cate and myself, is her looping handwriting on the back of that photo I'd found hidden inside Cate's own bathroom all those years ago.

Catie and Jim.

My fingers grab something at the bottom of the bag.

Two things, really. I pull them out.

They aren't pictures.

Of course they aren't.

The first item is a ratty piece of fabric, small, worn, grayed with age and time and God knows what else. Grimacing, I hold it up to the light. There's a silkiness beneath the grime. I realize what it is, and my mouth goes dry. It's *Pinky*.

A literal piece of my childhood.

I smooth the blanket's frayed stitching with my thumb. I don't know how or why Cate had this, but I also don't remember the last time I saw it, which is strange. It's like, Pinky was important to me and then it wasn't, and that makes me feel sad. And selfish. Like, what else have I forgotten about because I don't need it anymore?

"Sorry, Pinky," I whisper.

Pinky doesn't answer.

I shift my attention to the second item, which is bigger. It's a book. A paperback book.

I turn it around and right side up to get a look at the title.

What the ever-loving hell, Cate?

It's a play by Sophocles. Well, three of his plays, apparently: *Antigone, Oedipus the King,* and *Electra.*

Sophocles?

I get up and walk to unlock the bathroom door. I peek out.

My lungs deflate with relief. Angie isn't standing there, waiting to concern-pounce or ship my ass off to one of those troubled-teen schools you see advertised in the backs of magazines. My room is empty. I slink over to my desk, where I switch on a light to inspect the book more closely.

The words "Ventura Youth Correctional Facility" are stamped in purple ink on the inside cover. Stolen property, apparently, which feels like it should be funny only I'm not in the mood to laugh. On the opposite page, someone's scrawled the words "fuck this shit fuck motherfucker," and given what I know about Oedipus, I'm not sure whether that's irony or literary criticism.

I go to flip through the yellowed pages, and something slips from the book. Right onto my foot. I stoop to pick up what turns out to be an index card. A makeshift bookmark, I guess, only I have no idea what it had been marking. I squint as I straighten up and hold it under the light. There, written in blue ballpoint pen on the bottom left of the card, is the message:

just so you know . . .

What? Know what? I have no idea what this means. But Cate definitely wrote it. No doubt about that. I'd recognize her scribbly handwriting anywhere—besides, she always dots her *j*'s with *x*'s. Like she's wishing death on anyone who might dare to read what she has to say.

I skim the rest of the pages, looking for margin notes or messages, *anything* that might give me a clue as to what this book has to do with me or what Cate's trying to say. I'm not all that familiar with Sophocles. I mean, yeah, I remember Oedipus because we read about him in ninth grade, and who can forget a guy who kills his dad, bangs his mom, then pokes his own eyes out? That's pretty much a hot-mess trifecta, right there. Antigone I don't know a thing about, but that same ninth-grade English teacher did tell us Electra was supposed to be the female equivalent of Oedipus, so maybe she gets it on with her dad or does something equally gross. Like kills her mom.

I keep flipping.

I keep looking.

For something.

For meaning.

But there's nothing.

Just tragedy.

THIRTY-SEVEN

Monday morning, I come up with a plan.

It's a plan that quickly gets derailed when it starts to rain again and I have to tape up Dr. No's broken rear window with a sheet of plastic and duct tape.

Predictably the plastic leaks. I wrestle with it on the side of the road on my way to school and end up soaked. The whole thing's a lost cause, so I ditch out on my early classes and drive straight to an auto body shop to get the glass replaced. The guys working there take one look at the brick in the back and ask if I've called the cops or filed an insurance claim. This sounds like a total hassle and an even further derailment from my Plan, so I tell them I'll pay out of pocket to have it fixed.

"Must be nice to have parents with money, huh, kid?" The guy who takes my credit card looks like he wants to throttle me.

"You want to switch?" I snap back. I feel surly. I'm not in the mood for his poor-little-rich-boy mockery. It's not like I haven't heard it before, but the Henry wealth is something I refuse to feel guilty about. Why should I? I mean, I gave up a lot to live with my parents, and I sure as hell didn't have any say in the matter.

I walk over to the candy machine and jam a quarter in. A bunch of sour chewies spill into my hand. I stick them in my mouth one by one while I wait.

Above an oil-stained couch is a wall map. I peer at it, tracing my finger from Danville all the way out to Richmond. When I woke up this morning, I decided it was where I needed to go. That's my Plan. I found the address of where my mother, Cate, and I all lived together. It was written on my mother's death certificate, and if Cate can't or won't tell me what it is she knows about her, maybe I can figure it out on my own. It's not like Cate has any more of a right to this knowledge than I do. No matter what she says.

It's time to end this dysfunctional canon of ours. I decided that, too. This maddening refrain of me after her. For the first time ever, I'm going to play outside the chords.

I am my own force.

I can have my own vision.

I need to believe that.

Jenny finds me at the water fountain in the main classroom building some time before fourth period. I don't know how long I've been there. Minutes. Hours. *Days.*

"Save some for the rest of us," she says, and my heart's thumping before I look up because I instantly recognize her voice.

Jenny smiles her sun-in-winter smile at me and leans her shoulder against the wall. She's got purple sparkle rain boots on and this tight gray sweater that hugs her body in ways that make my brain go kind of nuts. I don't want to be *that* guy, though, so I straighten up quickly. And stare into her eyes.

I want to lose myself in those eyes.

She lets me.

Standing in the school hallway with Jenny, this girl I like so damn much, I'm flooded with my familiar sad-because-I'm-happy feeling. I don't get why this is, but you know, there you go.

"Hey," I say softly.

"Hey," she replies. "Where were you this morning?"

"Fixing my car."

"It was broken?"

"Yeah. And it was still broken after I tried fixing it myself. Had to get professional help and everything."

Her head tilts. "This is a metaphor for something, isn't it?"

"Most definitely."

She reaches out and takes my hand. Pulls me to her. "Well, it's good to see you again."

"Indeed."

"What happened here?" she asks.

I look down. Her finger is tracing a cluster of small, scabbed wounds that line the back of my hand and wrist. I tug at my jacket sleeve to cover the marks and give a loose shrug. "I don't know what happened. I forget."

She frowns and pulls me closer. Our hips are almost touching. Behind her, I see Hector Ramirez stroll out of the guy's bathroom. He looks over at us. I stare at him for the briefest of moments.

"Jenny," I say. "Will you go somewhere with me?"

"Now or later?"

"Now."

"But you just got here."

I take her other hand in mine. "I know. But it's important."

There's a moment of hesitation. I don't know if that's about me or her, but then Jenny nods and her deep brown eyes are shining. With trust.

God, I hope it's trust.

We start walking to the exit door.

"Where are we going?" she asks as we step outside into the rain.

"To a place from my past."

THIRTY-EIGHT

Jenny and I make out in the back of the Jeep before we hit the road. I try to be gentle with her, not ask for too much, but that's easier said than done when she's the one pushing me against the seat, crawling on top of me, pinning me down with her hips and her heat. I can tell she likes knowing how she drives me crazy, but when she fingers the button of my jeans, that's when I pull back. Her boldness sets off my worrying thing. It's dumb, but I can't help it. I start thinking maybe she's done this before. With some other guy. Or maybe other guys want to do this with her, and I won't be good enough at it to keep her interest. Or maybe she needs me to be the strong one. I'm not Cate and I won't let her be. It'd be easy to get carried away, it really would, but this is too fast. Too soon. It feels dangerous. I mean, we're in the school parking lot, of all places.

My head's still spinning when I sit up. Jenny stares at me, chest heaving, hair all in her face, and it's like my pulling away's the last thing she expects. Or wants.

I know better than to tell her what it is I'm thinking, so I cup her chin in my hand and kiss her quickly on the lips.

"We should get going," I say. "Before there's too much, you know, traffic."

Jenny laughs. It's a strong sound, like a ringing bell.

It grounds me.

The drive to Richmond's a long one, almost an hour, and I've already explained where we're going. And why. Jenny sits and plays with the music on my phone. She's looking for something to listen to. My shoulders, which felt loose and relaxed when I first slid behind the wheel, grow tighter with each passing mile. I squeeze my hands open and shut to release tension.

"Ugh," Jenny says.

"Ugh, what?"

"Your music. It's all angsty boy stuff."

This gets me to smile. "What'd you expect? Happy girl stuff?"

"I don't know. You're a musician. I expected something *good*."

"Put Jobim on," I tell her. "You'll like it."

"That's jazz, isn't it?"

"Latin jazz. Just put it on."

She does. Warm guitar chords fill the car, and a rush of painful longing fills my chest. Jenny wasn't wrong about the angsty thing.

"Your car reeks, you know," she says. "Like an ashtray."

"That's the cost of having chain-smoking mechanics work on it." I flip on the air and pray Jenny doesn't ask why I took the Jeep to the shop in the first place.

"God, it's so terrible about your mom." She stares out the window as she says this. The hills on both sides of us are green, lush. Grateful for the rain. "I had no idea about any of that."

I shrug.

"I didn't even know you were adopted. I think that's pretty interesting. Adoption."

"Interesting?"

"Yeah, sure. Who doesn't fantasize about not being related to their parents? Parents are everyone's worst nightmare. They wear Crocs. They refer to Chipotle as 'Cha-pottle.' They think having 'Me So Horny' as their ringtone makes them cool."

I can't help but laugh. "Things could be a lot worse, believe me."

"Oh, don't get me wrong. I love my parents. I do. It's just, no one wants to look at them and feel like they're looking into the future, you know?"

Well, no, I don't know. But I do like that she's telling me. "I'll take your word for it."

Soon the green hills are gone, and the traffic slows. On the right, out Jenny's window, the San Francisco Bay is visible, but the tall smokestacks of an oil refinery blight the view. We've entered Richmond city limits. Jenny leans back against her seat and gazes up at an enormous roadside billboard advertising a cemetery whose main selling point appears to be its proximity to an auto mall.

"So where's your mom buried?"

"I don't know," I say.

"You don't know?"

"Nope." I try to sound casual, but we've just passed the sign for the exit I want, only a quarter mile more, and it's suddenly hard for me to breathe. I rub at my chest, pressing down on the space between my ribs.

I feel Jenny looking at me.

"You okay?"

"Yeah."

"You look upset. Shit. I shouldn't have asked that about your mom. I swear, I lack some sort of sensitivity gene. I do realize this."

"Nah, it's fine. I'm good. Really."

Jenny nods, relaxing, and it's like last week when my parents told me that Cate had been set free—I'm relying on the fact that it's what I say that counts.

Not what I'm thinking.

This is all too much for me.

Any more stress, and I'm going to lose my damn mind. . . .

The deeper we get into Richmond, the more I regret bringing Jenny along. No, she doesn't need my rescuing, but that doesn't mean I want to be the one to put her in danger. And this place is downright scary. It's a type of poverty and ruin I've never seen before.

Except, you know, I have.

Making the whole experience exponentially worse is the fact that this grungy, industrial city is impossible to navigate by car. None of the streets run at right angles, and GPS is no help. I keep crossing over train tracks, turning down dead ends, and every time I have to back the Jeep up, I spy clumps of people loitering on every corner, even in the rain. They watch us with a cool sort of curiosity and a cruel sort of resentment. My arms start to itch under the weight of their gaze. Is this who I would've become if my mother hadn't died? I don't have an answer to that question. Or hell, I guess I do. Because growing up in Danville with the Henrys, I've always understood that when you're adopted, your successes are chalked up to nurture. But the bad stuff, like arson and assault charges, well, those things are all nature, baby.

In other words, sometimes fate is what other people make of it.

I don't like that. At all.

"You want me to ask for directions?" Jenny points to a corner store with a handwritten sign that reads: JUG LIQUOR: NOW OPEN! "What's a Jug Liquor?"

Oh, Lord. I slow down, squinting through the *thwap thwap* of the windshield wipers. "Are those bullet holes in the wall?"

"I don't know." Jenny fingers the door handle. "Let me out."

"You stay in the car," I say quickly. "I'll go ask."

She crosses her arms. "I'm capable of asking for directions, you know."

"I know that! But just . . . stay, all right?"

"Fine."

I walk into the liquor store, rain rolling down my nose and cheeks, and the musty scent of corn nuts and wet dog hits me all at once. The slumbering form of a German shepherd in the corner solves part of that mystery, and I breathe a sigh of relief that I haven't stepped into the middle of an armed robbery or something. There's still time, I suppose, but everything looks pretty normal. Customers swarm all over the place.

Anxiety still sky-high, I sneak a glance at the front counter. A tall black man in a Santa hat and navy peacoat is staring right back at me, arms folded, thin lips pressed tight in disapproval. Damn it. I duck out of sight and quickly grab a can of soda and a bag of Circus Peanuts even though I'm not hungry. I swear, something about me arouses suspicion wherever I go. I'd told Cate that once, and she was wholly unsympathetic.

"You're just paranoid," she said. "It's a self-fulfilling prophecy."

I go up to the counter to pay. The tall man keeps staring. Despite my self-fulfilling whatever, I wonder if it's my whiteness that sticks out here. I don't doubt it. Cate's never understood stuff like that—the fact that perception and perspective can be stronger forces than reality. When we were younger, we used to lie side by side in the grass beneath the Danville summer sun. She'd hold her tanned arm up to my paler one and fantasize about her absent father, wondering aloud whether she had the blood of an African prince or a Mayan warrior running through her veins. I always thought that was dumb and told her so. Whatever she was or wasn't on the inside didn't matter. She was white enough on the outside to believe being anything else might make her life more interesting.

"Um, can you tell me where Barrett Street is?" I ask the Santa hat man.

"You sure you don't mean Barrett Avenue?"

I pull out my mom's death certificate to check. "It says street."

He frowns even more, and I wonder if he knows what kind of document I'm holding. Finally he reaches under the counter and pulls out a map, not on his phone, but a paper one that's tattered and faded. We spend a few moments staring at it together. Barrett Street appears to run adjacent to the oil refinery. The one with the blight-making smokestacks.

"What're you going there for, kid?" he asks.

"I—I used to live there."

The lines in his face smooth out. He looks almost sad. "You lived there?"

"Yeah."

He nods out the smudged-up window. "And now you got that nice Jeep out there and a fine little girl with you?"

A flush of shame-heat washes over me, and it's like I've been caught trying to be someone or something I'm not. "Yeah," I say again.

He shakes his head. "Then why the hell would you ever want to go back?"

THIRTY-NINE

"I'm getting out now, Jamie. And so are you."

We've been sitting in front of the Barrett Street house for ten minutes, and Jenny's gone through practically the whole bag of Circus Peanuts. I sort of can't believe her. I'm pretty sure I'd throw up if I tried to swallow one. I might throw up anyway, which is not only a testament to how awful I feel, but I think it says something about Circus Peanuts.

Ducking around Jenny's arm, I stare at the house again. It's bigger than I would've guessed. Two stories of leaning brown stucco with a flat asphalt roof and a front yard filled with white sparkly rocks. No plants. Just rocks. Like an alien landscape. "I don't understand why I can't remember it. I mean, not at *all*."

"A lot of people can't remember stuff from when they were a kid."

I sit back. "Oh, yeah? What's your first memory?"

Jenny squirms in her seat and takes another bite of foam candy peanut. "I was riding on my dad's shoulders as he walked me to pre-school. It was spring and there were blossoms on the apple trees, and I grabbed for them. This was back when we lived in Monterey."

"How old were you?" I ask.

"Four."

I blow air through my cheeks. "I lived here until I was almost *six*."

"Well, what's your first memory, then?"

"I . . . I sort of remember my mother. But I only remember certain things. Impressions. Like the warmth of the bed we shared, me on one side of her, Cate snoring on the other. Like the sweet, sweet scent of her cigarettes on her clothes. Or the soft way her dark hair would tickle me when she wanted me to laugh. I remember other things, too. Bad things. Like the drugs and the men and—"

Jenny touches my shoulder. "Hey."

I look at her. "Only those aren't memories of events, are they? They're just *things*. Feelings."

"Yeah, but there's something in the way you talk about her. It's kind of—"

"Kind of what?"

"Intense."

"Wanting to remember my mom *is* intense."

She softens. "I'm sure it is. What's the first event you remember?"

I close my eyes. Force myself back in time. "I was in a group home with Cate after our mom died. There were spiders on the floor and I was scared, so she snuck a Pop-Tart out of the kitchen and brought it to me."

"That's sweet."

My eyes fly open. "But I was six then! Why can't I remember things from earlier?"

"You think something bad happened to you? Something that made you forget?"

"Well, I know it did. My mom got shot. Right in front of me! I know it's normal to forget traumatic stuff like that, and maybe that explains why I can't remember anything from before, but . . ."

"But?"

I drop my gaze. Inspect the cup holder between the seats. "Sometimes I still forget things."

"What do you mean?"

"Like I don't remember pulling out my eyebrows. And then there are other times that . . ." I shake my head. I can't tell Jenny about passing out in the Peet's parking lot. I just can't. It's too mortifying.

God.

"Other times I just don't know," I say.

"Get out of the car," she tells me.

The barking starts before we even reach the cyclone fence, freight-train loud. I freeze, then take a step back as a monster dog comes charging down the driveway, right at us. It skids on all fours and crashes against the fence. White rocks and slobber go flying. There's a gleam of teeth. The dog's a pit bull, brindle and white, and it's got this enormous head that barks and barks and barks. I want to clap my hands over my ears, but instead I do an about-face, twisting my shoulders so that I'm facing the street again.

I start walking away. Quickly.

"Hey!" Jenny calls after me. "Hey!"

She grabs my arm and turns me around.

"It's okay," she says. "You can do this."

There's acid stinging the back of my throat and I'm shivering inside the rain parka I have on, but I nod.

Jenny marches us back up the steps toward the house. The monster dog continues to bark. Like Cujo or Beethoven or whatever that man-eating movie dog is called.

"Shh, boy," she says, tucking hair behind her ear and leaning forward.

My heart lurches. "Jenny, stop that!"

"Oh, he's not mean. Just loud. Look." She holds a hand out, puts it right against the fence, like a sacrificial offering. The dog sniffs it wildly.

I swear he wants blood. "Don't!"

She glances over her shoulder. "You're scared of dogs?"

"No! I just don't like them."

"You look scared," she says.

I scowl.

The front door of the house opens. An old lady with gray-brown skin and gray-brown hair sticks her head out. She doesn't say anything. She just stares.

"Maybe we should go," I mutter. "I don't want to get shot."

"Jamie!"

"Or mauled by a rabid pit bull."

"You're being awful. Seriously. We came all this way—"

I raise my voice. "These are perfectly valid concerns. Seeing as my mother DIED. Right here!"

"Who died?"

I look up to see the old lady creeping down the steps to the cracked cement walkway that's slick with rain. She's wearing a black tracksuit, and there's a baseball cap with an elephant on it perched atop her head. The dog swirls around her legs. I hold my stomach and bend over. Yeah, I get it. I'm being awful. But I'm also pretty sure I'm going to vomit. Right here. On Jenny's purple sparkle boots.

Jenny throws me an exasperated look. Then she turns back to the woman. "Do you know where apartment B is?"

Old lady hand goes to old lady ear. "Heh?"

"Apartment B! This address."

"No apartment B, hon. Who're you looking for? Who died?"

"His mom. Her name was—"

"Amy Nevin," I manage to say.

The woman gasps. Monster dog notices. It gives a low growl and drops its head.

"You're Amy's boy?" she says. "My God."

"Yeah," I say, still clutching my stomach. "I am. I'm Amy's boy."

"This your sister?"

"Oh. No. This is my friend, Jenny. I'm Jamie."

The old woman nods. "You were called Jimmy back then, you know."

Now my eyes sting. But I'm able to stand. "I think I did know that."

"You come here to relive old times?"

Jenny speaks up. "He doesn't remember his mom. He thought maybe coming here would help him remember."

"You don't remember her?"

"Not really. Just a few things."

"I see."

"So you were here then?" I ask.

"I sure was. In and out. But this house has been in my family for sixty-four years. We used to rent out the basement, for cheap, you know, to help good folks who needed it. Like Amy. Only no one's lived there . . . since. That's why I didn't know what you were talking about with apartment B. There is no apartment B. There really never was."

"Do you think we could see it?" Jenny asks. "The basement?"

The old woman's lips purse. She looks right at me. "That something you want to do, Jimmy?"

"Jamie," says Jenny.

"Still the same person, isn't he? Doesn't matter what he's called."

"It *does* matter," Jenny insists.

"Yes," I say quickly. "Yes, I'd like to see it. If that's okay."

The woman gives a deep sigh, then reaches up for the gate latch with one hand, while holding on to her dog's collar with the other. "Sure it's okay. I'm Darlene, by the way. Get down, now, Hippo. These are good kids. You don't have to worry. They won't bite."

FORTY

I've never seen anything sadder than the basement of 356 Barrett Street. It consists of two cinderblock-walled rooms, with water pipes running across the ceiling and a foul-looking bathroom. The windows are cracked. The air is frigid, and I see no sign of a heat source other than a hot water heater mounted in the corner that has a pan of rusty water pooling beneath it. The floor is a cement pad and exposed insulation sticks out from the walls. Probably asbestos, and I don't think that's hyperbole on my part. Even Jenny looks freaked out. She's crouched in a corner by a cracked sink with one arm wrapped around Hippo's neck. The dog is licking her face.

I pace the perimeter of the room, peering into corners, running my hands over surfaces. I've already seen it all, but I need to keep moving. I need to do something to keep from breaking down.

I *lived* here.

Cate, I think madly. *This is terrible. Why can't I remember this place? Why I can't remember anything?*

What have you seen that I haven't?

What did that do *to you?*

"Darlene?" I ask.

"Yes, dear?"

"What did my mom look like?"

"She was just a girl, hon. Not much older than you are now. She was a pretty thing. Too pretty. You really don't remember her?"

I shake my head. "I have flashes. Like I know she had black hair like Cate. But long, like down her back. And I think she had skinny knees. She smoked, I know that, too."

Darlene holds a hand up. "Whoa, whoa, that's not right at all. Your mama was a blonde. Waifish, too. Like your girl here. Don't think she smoked, either, least not in the house. I'd remember that. Ron—that's my nephew—he's got asthma, so we've always been careful. Couldn't fix the air outside, but inside, we did the best we could. But Amy was a lovely thing. A dear. And she was funny, too. Her laugh could make anyone smile. Except you. You were a very serious child, Jimmy. Your sister, though, she was like Amy. Happy. A joy to be around."

I feel like I've been punched.

"My mom was *blond*?"

"Yes."

"Always blond? Or did she like, dye it?"

"Blond for as long as I knew her. You must get that brown hair from your daddy. You've got her lips, though. They're his best feature, don't you think?"

Jenny nods and smiles.

My heart stutters. "D-do you know who my dad is?"

"No, I'm sorry. Amy never said."

I slump. "Well, did she, you know, was she with a lot of men?"

Darlene frowns. "Where'd you hear that?"

"I thought I remembered it. That she had men over. I always wondered if that was part of how she died. If one of the guys she knew did it. Killed her." And covered it up. Made it look like an accident.

"You don't know who did it?"

I shake my head.

She scratches at her chin and neck. "I see."

"Do you know?" Jenny asks.

The look Darlene shoots Jenny isn't a friendly one, but she warms when she turns back to me. "What I know is that Amy Nevin was a sweet girl who was in over her head. Twenty-four. No money. Two kids on her own. I don't know every detail about how she lived or how she died, but I know she loved you, Jimmy, okay?"

I nod, but my knees feel weak. My heart, too. Thoughts and questions rumble inside me, desperate ones like *Why didn't you take us in? Why did we go to strangers? We didn't need private school or riding lessons. We needed someone to want us. My mother made you happy. My sister, too. Wasn't that enough?*

But the voice inside my head is there, quick as truth, whispering: *You didn't make her happy, though, did you? You were no joy to be around. She practically said as much.*

I bite my lip.

Darlene watches me. "How's your sister doing?" she asks.

"Not well. She got in some trouble a few years back."

"Sorry to hear it. Worst thing there is, worrying about kids." She lights up. "You know, I might have a few items of your mother's upstairs. You want to me to go check?"

I nod again. "Do you think you could leave, uh, Hippo, outside?"

"Sure thing, hon."

Ten minutes later Darlene comes back down into the basement. Jenny's sitting on the edge of the crumbling cinderblock wall looking at her phone. I'm pacing.

"I'm sorry," she says. "I thought I had a few things of hers. I know I did because I cleaned this place out. Nothing valuable, but some small items, those stone statues."

"Statues? Of what?"

"One was a tiger. The other was . . . I can't remember. Another animal, I think. I had them in storage for a while, but I forgot that woman came and got them."

Disappointment slips over me like a suit of armor. "What woman? Angie? That's my mom. The one who adopted me."

"I don't know her name. It was a white lady with curly hair. Sort of heavyset. With glasses."

I freeze. Definitely not Angie. But what comes to mind is a long-ago car ride. Driving with the windows down, clutching Pinky in one hand and Cate in the other, while a bubbly woman smoked menthols and told us how lucky we were to have found parents whose children had died.

"Was it a social worker? The one who handled our adoption?"

Darlene shrugs. "Well, now that might be right. I don't really re-member. That would make sense, though, wouldn't it? But that would mean the folks who took you in should have her stuff."

FORTY-ONE

On the drive back, the rain starts up again as soon as we pass the cemetery.

"You okay?" whispers Jenny.

"I don't know," I say. "I'm sorry. I shouldn't have brought you. That was weird."

"Well, I'm glad you did. Bring me. You wouldn't have wanted to go alone."

A headache has taken root in the base of my skull. It's sprouting into something prickly and fast-growing. Something beyond my control.

"You're right," I say. "I wouldn't have wanted to go alone."

"So what does that mean? No one seems to know anything about your mother."

I look at her, face shadowed with sheets of rain. "I don't think—"

"You don't think what?"

My voice lowers to a whisper. "I don't think my mom is who I thought she was."

"Jamie . . ."

"Jenny, *listen*. Look, I remember a woman with long dark hair. But the woman Darlene described—that wasn't her."

"So who was it?"

"I don't know."

"And where's the woman you remember?"

"I don't know that, either!"

"Jamie?"

"What?"

Jenny pauses. "You don't think your mom could still be alive, do you?"

My hands squeeze the steering wheel so tightly my knuckles go white.

My hands, my hands, my hands . . .

"Don't say that," I whisper. "Please. I can't even go there. I don't know what I think. I don't know *anything*."

"Do your parents, the ones you live with, do you think they have those items Darlene was looking for?"

"I've never seen them. They've never mentioned having them."

"That doesn't mean they don't."

"No . . . but there's one person I want to ask about that."

"Your sister?"

I shake my head. "No, not her."

FORTY-TWO

That night, I'm sitting on the floor of my room watching a bad movie about the end of the world when the phone rings.

It's almost eleven, and I've been up here for hours, ever since dropping Jenny off at her chamber group. When I got home, I had too many questions for Angie and Malcolm that I knew they'd never answer, so I just mumbled something about feeling like crap and came upstairs. You'd think they'd take a hint, but of course, Angie's already knocked once to remind me about an appointment with Dr. Waverly tomorrow afternoon. Then she knocked *again* five minutes later to make sure I heard her the first time. Fifteen minutes after *that*, she sent Malcolm up to see if I "needed anything." Now my headache has swelled to apocalyptic proportions, so it sort of *does* feel like the end of the world when my sister calls.

I pick it up anyway.

"Hey," I say wearily.

"What's wrong with you?" Cate snaps.

"I think I'm sick." I reach to mute the movie I'm watching, so I don't have to strain to hear her over the sound of exploding buildings and panicked crowds.

"How sick?" she asks.

"I don't know. I have a headache. A bad one. Maybe it's a migraine."

"You got those as a kid, remember? They'd get so bad they'd make you puke."

"No, I don't remember that," I say. "At all. Cate, are you watching me?"

"What do you mean? Why would I do that?"

"I feel like someone's watching me. At night. All the time, even."

"You sound paranoid, Jamie."

"Do I? Because I'm not paranoid if I'm right, you know. If you really are watching me."

"Wow, you're, like, so deep right now."

I stare out the window. The rain's stopped, but the wind's still blowing. Pounding, actually. "Alarms keep going off near the house. And the Dunnings got broken into on Friday. It was in the paper."

"Am I supposed to give a shit?"

"I thought you might."

"Well, you thought wrong. Again."

"Why'd you run away from me the other day?"

"*I* didn't run away. You did."

"What?"

"You held your breath until you passed out. I kind of took that to mean our conversation was over."

I feel the swift knock of panic rushing to fill my soul. "I don't remember doing that."

"Mmm, you don't say."

"Cate, I think there's something wrong with me. Really wrong. I've been pulling my eyebrows out again. My cataplexy's getting worse, too. Three times in the last week."

"You don't have cataplexy, Jamie."

"What?"

"I said you don't have cataplexy."

"Yeah, well, what do I have, then?"

"It's a convert—conversion something. Shit. I forget."

"A conversion? Like being born again?"

"No! Double shit. Hell, don't ask me. I'm not a doctor!"

Unbelievable. "Where are these pictures of our mom? You said you'd give them to me. You *promised*."

She sniffs. "Things change, little brother. It's the way of the world."

A flush of anger runs through me. Why did I ever help her in the first place? Burying her things in the woods and sparing her even worse punishment? Why? She's not crazy. She's *cruel*.

I sit up, gripping the phone. "I went to the house where we used to live, you know. Out in Richmond. The woman there said our mom had blond hair. That's not what I remember. Our mom had dark hair, right?"

She says nothing.

"Cate?"

"Yeah?"

"Did you hear what I asked?"

"I heard you. You're practically screaming."

I am definitely *not* screaming. "Why doesn't our mom look like how I remember her?"

"Maybe you only remember what you want to. Maybe that's your goddamn problem."

"I—" I know what I'm going to ask might upset her. I know it might set her off. But I have to do it. "I've been trying to remember a lot of things lately. Things from the past. And that time I rode your horse down at the barn, after I held my breath, did you . . . hypnotize me?"

Silence.

"Cate?"

"Maybe I did," she whispers. "And maybe I should have done it again. Only I didn't. Instead I bought into the lie that what you don't know can't hurt you. But it can, Jamie. It can hurt bad. You'll figure that out on your own, though. I know you will. You're so close. Now *go deeper.*"

FORTY-THREE

The following morning finds me lurking around the parking lot of the Happy Homes Adoption Agency in Stockton, which is a downtrodden delta town more than sixty miles northeast of Danville. It's early still, and I barely remember the drive out here—the whole trip's a hazy blur of bad heartburn, brake lights, and gas station coffee. So far, I've been passing time by doing jumping jacks to the beat of Ellington's "Caravan," and generally looking like a crazy person. A painted mural of brightly colored flowers and brightly colored children adorn the wall behind me, and even though I've been freezing my butt off for over an hour in the crisp December air, it was a good call on my part, remembering the cigarettes. This is because when the back door of the agency opens and the woman I've been waiting for comes out, she makes a beeline straight for the ashtray I've positioned myself next to.

I stop jumping and watch as she approaches. It's been ten years, but I recognize her immediately, all the way down to the shiny pack of Kools and plastic lighter she's got gripped in one chubby hand. Her frizzy hair's cut short now, but she's still tall and sort of lumpy, and either there's something off about her makeup or there's just a whole lot of it.

"Hello, Miss Louise." I try keeping my voice steady, but breath and words spill together from my mouth in a jumbled rush.

The woman blinks. "How do you know who I am?"

"I recognized you."

"Well, tell me who you are then or I'll call the cops. You a relative?"

"A relative? Of who?"

"Of one of my kids."

I'm confused. "Your kids?"

The look in her eyes isn't wary so much as weary. She pulls a cigarette out. Lights it. "Not *my* kids. But mine, you know? The ones I work with."

"No," I say. "I'm not a relative."

"Well, then . . ."

"I think I *am* one of your kids."

Miss Louise takes a step toward me. Minty smoke leaks from her nostrils, lit-grenade style, and her lips start to stretch into a smile. "Yeah? What's your name, then? Bet I remember you. I remember all my kids, and I've been doing this job for over ten years."

"My name's Jamie. Jamie Henry."

Miss Louise freezes. Her soft dumpling skin goes white. Then *whiter.*

"Oh," she says.

I cock my head. "What's wrong? Don't you remember me?"

"Of course I remember you, Jamie. You . . . you're all grown now. But I heard about what happened with your sister. That was sad. Real sad. I'm sorry."

I nod quickly. My chest is doing its tightening thing again. "Thank you."

"How'd you find me?" she asks.

"Wasn't hard. I did a search for all the Louises that worked in adoption services. Found your picture on the Happy Homes website. Stockton's kind of far from Richmond, though."

"I didn't work here when I knew you. I was out in West County then. Social services."

"Oh."

"Is everything okay, Jamie?"

"I guess."

"Your parents treating you well? What was their name again?"

"The Henrys. Malcolm and Angie."

"Of course. The Henrys. Terrible what happened to their kids."

I lift my chin. "You mean their 'real kids,' right? That's what people call them, you know. Like Cate and I are imaginary."

"That's not what I meant at all. But what happened to them *was* terrible. You do understand that, right?"

My shrug is noncommittal. I mean, of course I understand, but I don't totally agree with the terrible part, which is one of those nasty truths that can fill me with the most sinister sense of badness. But maybe it's the way any child born or adopted after the death of a sibling feels, this queasy lurch from gratitude to shame; if Madison and Graham hadn't died, where the hell would I be? "Miss Louise, do you think I could ask you some questions? About when I was younger? And about my mom? My real mom."

She scratches the bottom of her chin with her thumb. " 'Real' mom, huh? Yeah, sure. Shoot."

My mouth goes dry.

"Sorry," she says. "That was tactless."

I manage to clear my throat. "Do you know what my mom looked like?"

"Nope. Never saw her."

"Well, after she died, did you ever go back to the house we lived in and get some of her things?"

She frowns and puffs harder. "Yeah, I did. Wasn't much to get, though."

"What was there?"

"Don't remember. Nothing valuable. Good thing, too. That neighborhood was not optimal, and that's putting it lightly."

"Were there statues? Animal statues? Is that what you picked up?"

"I don't know. There might've been. Why're you asking these questions, Jamie?"

"I'm trying to learn more about where I came from. My past, you know? I don't remember anything from before I went to live with the Henrys. Sometimes it feels like nobody *wants* me to remember."

"You don't remember anything?"

"Not really. All I know is what I've been told. That my mom was shot. That we were wards of the state until we got adopted. That they never found out who it was that killed her."

"I see." Miss Louise presses her lips together so hard a stream of ash breaks off, vanishing into the valley wind in an instant. "Well, here's what I know: You were miserable in that group home with your sister. Always sick and crying. You got nits and your hair fell out."

My cheeks burn. "I remember *that*."

"If you remember that, then maybe you shouldn't be worrying about before. Maybe it's now that matters. Your life with the Henrys."

"But I want to know where I came from! That's important, isn't it?"

"Your parents now love you. Isn't that more important?"

"I guess," I say, but I don't know. Maybe that's the unspoken truth of parents whose living children have come after ones who were lost—it's not that they don't love us, it's that they wish they never had to.

Miss Louise tips her head at me. Soft curls dance across pale cheeks. "Do you know how rare it is for older children to be adopted? Much less stay with a sibling? It was practically a miracle, what happened to you and your sister. And you don't question miracles."

"You don't?"

"Oh, no. There's no truth that can change who you are. But looking into the past, at things that happened a long time ago, that can hurt you. Your sister's proof of that. So stop. All right?"

But I can't stop, is what I want to say, but my teeth chatter too hard in the chilled Stockton air. I look away.

Miss Louise reaches out. Takes my hand. Squeezes it hard enough to hurt.

"Be a *good* boy," she says.

FORTY-FOUR

So why am I questioning miracles?

This is the drumbeat query that gallops through my mind, faster and faster, as I navigate the tight valley fog, winding out of Stockton, leaving behind Miss Louise and the wispy reek of her Kools. The distance between us may be increasing, but her wisdom, however murky, sticks with me. It fills me with self-doubt, a haggard sense of rootlessness. Like swimming in a cold lake at night and not knowing which way is up, I don't know what the right thing to do is.

And maybe that's just how Cate wants it.

Drops of moisture hit my windshield.

I switch on my wipers.

I drive full speed into the murkiness.

When I finally reach school, I don't head to my classes or the office or anywhere I'll be forced to concoct lame, stuttering excuses for my absence. Instead I seek solace in Jenny. In her body more than her words. That sounds selfish, I know, or shallow, but my intent is far from prurient. I just want to be close to her. I need her. And okay, maybe that *is* selfish, but I like to think she gets something out of being with me. She seems to, and I don't mean in a giving way. I mean in the taking.

Jenny does a lot of taking.

She's the one who grabs my hand when I show up at lunch period to crumple beside her, burying my face against her shoulder, to tell her where I've been and what I haven't learned. She's the one who drags me through the quad and up into the woods behind the school's organic garden, where she shoves me up against a bare wood storage shed, scrunches up her face, and presses her lips to mine. I like that she does this, not just for the obvious reasons. I like that she doesn't pet my hand or ask if I'm okay, when it's pretty clear that I'm not. I like that she doesn't encourage me to smile sweetly and tell bland lies in order to spare her feelings. I like her. Period.

The kiss between us starts out tender, achingly so, like maybe she thinks I'm fragile or on the verge of tears, which I sort of am. But it's not long before our kissing becomes something more, something urgent, each of us grasping at the other in a way that's frantic and hungry and grateful all at once.

Soon I'm not thinking about whether she's done this with other guys, or if they're better at it than me. The only thing I'm thinking about is how good it feels to be with her and how the briefest of moments can bring such infinite pleasure. I slide one hand up Jenny's shirt as she watches me, eyes half closed, a wry smile on her lips. She's not wearing a bra, and my fingers revel in the softness of her skin, the shape of her, the way she leans into my touch. I lower my head to kiss her more, to put my mouth around her—

"Classy," a voice says, and we leap apart, both of us scrambling to fix our clothing. I stand protectively in front of Jenny as Hector Ramirez sidles up the path with one smart-ass look on his smart-ass face. A beam of sunlight peeks through the cloud layer, lighting his dark hair with amber.

"What do *you* want?" I snap, embarrassed at both how hard I'm breathing and how angry I feel. Jenny brushes dust and tree dander from my back and shoulders. I reach to do the same for her.

Hector shrugs. "I don't *want* anything. But I happened to see you two come out here, and right after that, I saw old lady Briscoe take some new family on a tour of the place. I figured they were about five minutes away from discovering you *in flagrante delicto* and thought maybe you'd want me to give you a heads-up on that."

I tuck my shirt back in my pants and glance down the hillside. Sure enough, the school secretary is waddling through the wet grass with some stuffy-looking parents and their middle school kid in tow.

"Thanks for that, Hector." I take Jenny by the hand.

"Hey," he says before we can leave.

I look back at him. "What?"

"You hear about the fire out on Dove Lane this morning?"

"No. What fire?"

"Apparently someone used a bunch of M-80s to set the church Dumpster on fire. Burned a tree and part of the roof, too. Cops are going nuts right now trying to find out who did it."

"And you know this how?"

"Danny texted me."

"Danny?"

"Yeah, he's home for winter break now. Told him it kind of re-

minds me of stuff that used to happen around here, if you know what
I mean."

I tighten my grip on Jenny's hand. "Yeah, I know."

"Funny how that works, huh?"

"Not that funny. But thanks again for the heads-up. I appreciate it."

"No you don't," he says grimly. "But you should."

My sense of dread is palpable. Jenny and I walk arm in arm back down
the trail, but I can't stop twisting my head to look up at the mountain
and out over the rolling hills. I'm searching for signs, omens, anything. Smoke signals of my sister's ire.

We make it back to the main quad. Other students see us and stare.
I know they know that we're dating. Or together. Or something. I wonder if that makes them look at me differently, knowing there's someone
who doesn't judge me by what my sister did. Knowing there's someone
who likes me more than they do.

"You think Cate set that fire?" Jenny whispers.

"I don't know."

"But that's what you're worried about."

"Yeah."

"So call the cops."

"I can't."

"Why not?"

"What would I say? I don't know anything. I'd sound crazy."

"Come on."

I shiver. "I can't tell them what I can't explain. It's just a feeling I
have. That it's a warning from Cate. Or a message. But I don't know
what it means."

"It means she's destructive."

"Or self-destructive."

"Same thing."

My head is starting to hurt. I press my fingers to my temple. "I need to think about this more."

"What're you doing after school?" Jenny asks.

"I've got a doctor's appointment."

"After that?"

"Don't know. I'm not looking forward to going home tonight, I know that much. Did you have something else in mind?"

Jenny points the toe of her shoe into the ground. "My parents are out of town. I thought maybe you'd want to come over. Spend the night even. We could talk some of this out. Family drama shouldn't happen in a vacuum, you know?"

I stop walking. Play at stupefaction. "Wait. You're asking me to stay over? At your house?"

Her cheeks go pink. "Well, not like *that*."

I bend to catch her eye. "I know."

"Maybe a little like that," she admits.

Even in my doom-and-gloom state, I can't help but grin. Then I walk Jenny to her class. When we get there, I don't want to let her go.

"I'll see you tonight," I tell her. "I promise."

FORTY-FIVE

I arrive early for my appointment with Dr. Waverly, so I sit on the waiting room couch and try reading some of the book Cate gave me. With this choice comes the inevitable worrying—I *should* be doing homework because winter break is coming up and that means finals. And I *should* be preparing for my fifteen-minute presentation on the Jimmy Carter grain embargo in U.S. History that's due in class tomorrow. However, not only is hell having to give a fifteen-minute presentation on the Jimmy Carter grain embargo, but if I'm serious about deconstructing this so-called miracle life of mine and putting out any and all fires I may have helped spread, maybe homework shouldn't be my top priority right now.

So Sophocles it is.

I start with *Electra*. A few pages in, I'm reminded what it is I don't like about Greek tragedies—they're weird. They also have something in common with me in that they don't seem to say what they mean. From what I'm getting, though, Electra and some other people are angry about her father's murder and vow to avenge his death. After that, Electra does a lot of crying and scheming, and there's not so much in the way of action. This bores me. I do however make note of the fact that Sophocles's take on fate is far different from mine, what with all the oracles and premonitions.

I lose focus after a bit, so I lean back and close my eyes. Listen to the burbling of the fish tank and the hum of fluorescent lights.

Cate, I think. *Why are you doing this?*

I am not an oracle.

I am not your goddamn mind reader.

My reverie is short-lived. Sally June, Dr. Waverly's receptionist or bookkeeper or whatever, gets on the phone and it's obvious she's not happy with whoever's on the other end. The white noise machine sitting outside Dr. Waverly's office door is running so no one can hear what's being said inside, but I can hear Sally June loud and clear. She's fighting with somebody.

"Axis one, two nine six point three two. Gaf is forty-eight." There's a pause, then she says, "Forty-eight!" in an irritated sort of way. I crack my eyes open. Sally June's twirling purple-streaked hair around a pen and staring at her computer screen like it's done her wrong. She hangs up the phone with a huff.

"What was that about?" I ask.

Sally June blows air out of her cheeks. "Just trying to fix something billing code related. They've got it all screwed up on their end."

"Codes for patients?"

"For insurance companies. Coverage is dependent on the primary diagnosis. If they get the diagnosis wrong, well, they don't pay. Because they're assholes."

"So those numbers were a diagnosis?"

"Yup."

I sit up. "What's the diagnosis you just said? Two nine six point three two?"

Sally June shakes her head. "I can't talk to you about patient charts."

"Well, what's my diagnosis?"

"You need to ask Dr. Waverly that. Also, don't quote me on the asshole thing, okay?"

"But—"

"It's the law, Jamie."

I nod and slouch back down, but my hands close around the arms of the chair to the point of pain. I understand not sharing other people's information, but why should the law protect me from having information about myself? That doesn't make any sense. Unless maybe there's something so horribly wrong with me that no one wants to tell me. But then, what good is therapy if it involves secrets? Wasn't the whole point of *Oedipus Rex* to *know thyself*?

I'm pretty damn sure it was.

"Here," Sally June says, standing up and walking over to a bookshelf adjacent to the waiting area. She pulls a large silver book off and hands it to me. I half expect to see the name Sophocles printed on the front, but instead it reads *Diagnostic and Statistical Manual of Mental Disorders*.

"What's this?" I ask.

"Book of codes. Knock yourself out, kid."

"Thanks."

Before she goes to sit back down, Sally June jogs over to the white noise machine and turns it on high. This time when she makes a phone call, I can't hear a thing.

I lean forward as I crack open the big silver book and start to flip through it. Sally June's right. In the index are tons of codes. Some are for psychological conditions I've heard of before, things like social phobia and schizophrenia and eating disorders, but there's also a whole section on sexual dysfunctions. I can't help but take a glance at these. Who wouldn't? They've got everything listed from sexual sadism to premature ejaculation, and I can't exactly imagine the circumstances under which I'd want to talk to Dr. Waverly about any of these issues. If I had any of these issues, I mean.

Which I totally don't.

After some hunting around, I spot the entry that reads 296, which is listed as Major Depressive Disorder. I turn to the page that describes this condition, and damn, it's depressing to read about depression. Not eating. Not sleeping. Not finding pleasure in things previously found pleasurable. Sounds like they've nailed it. My heart patters with lightning-strike curiosity. What was it Cate said was wrong with me last night? A *convert* something. I flip back to the index and run my finger down the page, looking for . . .

I blink and hold my breath.

There it is.

300.11 Conversion Disorder.

What *is* that?

"Jamie?"

I look up.

Dr. Waverly is smiling at me.

"You can come in now."

I sit in the black leather chair. I count the clocks.

Five. There are exactly five clocks in this room.

Dr. Waverly settles across from me. Adjusts her glasses. "So how are things?"

I let my fingers tap against my knees, releasing an uneven bass line of nerves. "Did you hear about what happened on Dove Lane this morning?"

"No, what happened?"

"Someone lit the Dumpster in the church parking lot on fire."

"I see."

"It's the church my family goes to."

"Is that why you mentioned it?"

"I mentioned it because it's bothering me."

"The fire's bothering you?"

"Yes!"

"How so?"

"I don't know how," I say, because like I told Jenny earlier, it's just a feeling I have. Feelings aren't always easy to explain. Even to a shrink.

Dr. Waverly clears her throat. "Well, I've received a few phone calls from your parents. Do you think we could talk about that?"

My parents? "Yeah, sure."

"They're worried about you. They told me you've been spending all your time locked in your bedroom lately. That you've been moody and irritable, lashing out whenever they try to speak with you. That you're not going to class."

I stare at the floor. Feel the back of my neck grow warm. "Oh."

"Is your anxiety bothering you again?"

"Not really. Not like before."

"Well, they also said you brought a girl home in the middle of the night, that you got sick all over your car and broke a window, along with some things in your bathroom. Is this right?"

"I . . . I guess."

"That doesn't sound like you."

I shake my head. I don't know what else to say. If I did something, then it *is* me. By definition.

"Are you using drugs?" Dr. Waverly asks gently.

I look up. "No!"

"Or drinking? I know we've talked about the importance of not mixing alcohol with your Prozac—"

"I'm not even taking the stupid Prozac," I mutter.

"What was that?"

"I stopped taking it last week. I hated it."

"I see."

I resent the way she says those words. *I see.* Like she knows me better than I know myself.

"What's a conversion disorder?" I ask.

"A conversion disorder? It's a type of psychosomatic condition. Jamie, look, you can't just stop taking medication like that. There can be bad side effects. Confusion. Rebound depression—"

"But I didn't have depression to start with! And I don't know what that means. Psycho whatever you said."

"Psychosomatic. It means the mind is capable of impacting the body. For some people, when they're sad or anxious, they feel that way. But for other people, sometimes their sadness or anxiety is expressed physically. Like getting a headache or a stomachache."

"So a conversion disorder means getting a headache or a stomachache?"

She frowns. "That's what psychosomatic means. Physical symptoms manifested by psychic distress. Conversion disorders are more specific in that the patient displays severe or dramatic neurological symptoms, often linked to a past trauma. Say a woman tried to yell out to her husband before he was hit by a car, but wasn't able to; she might have bouts of muteness when triggered by things that remind her of the accident. She would literally be unable to speak. Sort of like a physical echo of pain. Think of it like a stuck memory."

"Is that what's wrong with me, then? Do I have a stuck memory?"

"Why do you ask that?"

"My hands keep going numb."

"It's happened again since I last saw you?"

"Three times in the last week."

"Since you stopped taking your Prozac."

Since Cate came back. "Yeah, I guess."

"And you think what happens to your hands might be the result of a conversion disorder? Not cataplexy?"

"My cataplexy isn't normal in the first place. And you've told me before it could be a stress reaction, not a real nerve thing."

She blinks. "True. Well, is there an event in your past that your numbness might be connected to?"

"Yes," I say. "There is."

Dr. Waverly leans forward. "What is it?"

I suck in air and think of fate. I think of bloody hands digging in the dirt to bury my sister's secrets. Of raw skin and even rawer emotion. It's on the very tip of my tongue to tell Dr. Waverly what I did, burying Cate's stuff like that, and about the phone and the texts and the whole murderous truth of what I know about my sister and why I feel so *bad* about it.

But I don't.

Because what I'm also thinking about is:

Does Cate know what *I* did?

Oh, God.

"I'm sorry," I say, and I get to my feet. The back of my heel bumps against the chair and comes close to tripping me. I grab for my backpack. "I need to go."

"Jamie, please. I don't think—"

"I'm sorry," I say again, but now I'm walking away. I have to leave. Dr. Waverly calls my name again, but I'm already at the door and there's nothing she can do to stop me.

FORTY-SIX

Cate knows.

    Cate knows I have a conversion disorder.

    Cate knows I buried evidence of what she did.

    Cate knows I know she tried to kill Sarah.

    Back out on the sidewalk, I march away from Dr. Waverly's office and the neat rows of Victorian cottages with all the grace of an ungreased windup toy. My limbs jerk and twitch and resist any sort of harmony. I don't understand this. I don't understand anything. When I buried Cate's things, I was so careful. No one saw. I made sure of that.

    So how does she know?

The way she knows everything, I guess. Magic. Persuasion. Brute force.

But what does it mean?

That's a question I don't have an answer for.

I pull my hands from my pockets and stretch them out in front of me.

"Are you really all in my mind?" I ask them. "Is that what this is about? Because yes, yes, I know I did something wrong. God, do I know that. But I am so, so sorry—"

"Who the hell are you talking to, kid?" Someone bumps my shoulder as they pass by. I shy strongly to my left, cheeks burning, then skitter forward with my head hunched down. I don't turn to see who it was. I don't care. I know I look crazy.

You're talking to your hands.

Yeah, okay. That *is* crazy.

But maybe, just maybe, all this time, they've been talking to *me*.

Next thing I know, I'm in my Jeep.

I'm driving toward the Ramirez ranch, and my phone's ringing. The syncopated rhythm of "Evidence" fills the car, only it's no longer mournful and no longer beautiful. It's taunting now, and I refuse to answer it. I won't talk to her. Not yet.

Instead I focus my attention on the breathing exercises I've been taught. The ones that are meant to keep me from snapping when my anxiety spins out of control. Like now.

Inhale for four.

Hold for four.

Exhale for eight.

Repeat.

There's an almost physical ache pulling at me as I head farther and farther into the valley. And away from Jenny. More than anything, I want to see her, feel her, experience more of her solace. But there's something I need to do first. Something I've needed to do for the past two years. Because if Cate knows I have a conversion disorder, then she *knows* I'm the one that took her bag.

So maybe this has all been about her needing to confess.

The muscles in my neck stretch catgut taut. Because the truth is Cate might feel guilty about a lot of things. Because giving me a book of Greek tragedies and having me unearth her buried secrets might only be the beginning of what she has to say. Because my sister could have more in common with the matricidal Electra than just a bad temper and a flair for the dramatic.

just so you know . . .

The ranch is up ahead. I twist the wheel to park Dr. No on the shoulder, but the Jeep's moving too fast. It jolts into the underbrush, leaves slapping against the windshield, before coming to rest not far from where I left my bike all those years ago. I get out and look around. Unlike then, I can't walk up to the front door and announce my arrival, so I'll have to cut through the woods on my own. Light rain starts to fall. I pull the hood of my jacket up over my head.

I jam my keys into my back pocket. Then I start hiking.

I don't know what I expect to find when I get there—an empty hole in the ground. Cops with their guns drawn. Cate waiting in the shadows, plotting an ambush.

Anything.

What I *don't* expect to find is nothing—an undisturbed patch of rain-soaked earth nestled amid swirling mist at the foot of a leaning eucalyptus tree I'd discovered the day I'd come across the monstrous truth about my sister. I'd run through the woods with evidence of her crimes in my arms, panting, past flora and fauna, leaping over trickling streams, trying to get as far off the beaten path as possible.

Then I'd ended up *here*. Among swaying trees on the far side of a meadow filled with briar bushes and three-pronged poison oak leaves that glistened wet with oil and the promise of pain. One of the trees stood stunted and malformed. Its branches didn't grow up toward the sun, but instead twisted and turned back in on itself, so that the whole structure looked like a sick kind of maze, one that bowed and barely cleared the ground, ruined by the weight of its own mass.

The perfect place to bury my sister's sins.

Lazy rain comes down harder. I fall to my knees and begin to dig. Like then, the only tools I have now are my own two hands. The dampness of the earth aids me, but rocks and grit bring up blisters and tear my skin. I break off a stick from the leaning tree and poke around with it to loosen up the clay pack beneath the topsoil.

Then I dig more.

About two feet down, my mud-caked, bleeding hands strike nylon. I pull the bag out, wiping it down as best I can. After two years the fabric itself has rotted; the fibers are frayed and blackened. But the waterproof lining still protects the contents. I rifle around. Everything's still there: the damning cell phone, long dead, the scorched gloves, the silver lighter, Cate's journal. The three books on hypnosis.

Deep Trance Hypnotism
Induction
Self-Hypnosis: A Guide to Mindful Self-Control

I squint. Well, that last title is strange, considering Cate didn't hypnotize *herself*. Her inductions were meant for others. Schoolgirls. Me, even. I mean, she was kind of brilliant that way.

Curious, I crack the spine and hunch forward over the pages to keep them from getting soaked. Water streams down my nose and chin. The ink is smeared slightly and the paper stock holds a musty smell, but I have no problem seeing the passages that have been highlighted, the notes scribbled in the margins.

unable to validate mem. recovery; sstr uncooperative
per freud, repression as defense mech.
induction attempt per tx protocol
brain abnormality possible?

I'm confused. The handwriting's foreign, and the language in these notes isn't Cate's. It's too full of sophistication, too void of emotion. I flip back to the inside cover of the book, and that's when I see it—a stamp, not unlike the purple one marking Cate's stolen Sophocles as belonging to the Ventura Youth Correctional Facility. Only this one reads: PROPERTY OF JANETTE WAVERLY, MD.

My jaw drops.

Apparently the Sophocles isn't the first book Cate has stolen.

I jam the books back inside the rotting nylon bag, ready to stuff everything into the backpack I've brought with me. A small object slips through a hole in the frayed threads from one of the front pockets. It lands at my feet, splattering mud across my shoes. I bend at the waist to pick it up. It's not something I've seen before.

It's a statue. A small one. Of a tiger.

Or a tigress.

I stare at the carving for a long time. Long enough that my legs begin to tremble and a tingling creeps into my gut, because the cheap craftsmanship and the small chips of crystal in the eyes are familiar. Very familiar. Not only is this Cate's power animal, but it's also a match to another animal statue I know. One I've seen on a regular basis for, oh, the past eight years or so.

The stone carved owl from Dr. Waverly's office.

What the hell is going on?

I push my hair back from my eyes.

My phone rings.

I answer it this time.

FORTY-SEVEN

"Cate?" I bark, leaning up against the base of a pine tree with the phone wedged into the hood of my jacket to keep water from dripping on it. "Cate, I found it all. I found everything."

"What's that, Jamie? What did you find? I can barely hear you."

I nearly choke. *"Mom?"*

Maybe she can't hear me, but Angie's words come through loud and clear. "James, where are you?"

I glance around at the mud-splattered bag, my mud-soaked clothing and shoes. "I'm nowhere. Just . . . out."

"Well, come home. We need to talk."

"Is this about leaving therapy early? Because—"

"You left therapy early?"

I pause. "Isn't that what you're calling about?"

"I am calling about the fact that the police showed up at the house this afternoon. Asking for you."

"The *police*? Why?"

"They're looking into something that happened out in Berkeley. Somehow your name came up. I told them they had the wrong person, but they insisted on talking to you."

"In Berkeley?"

"Something about a store being vandalized. There was *a fire*."

Something goes off in my head. Very faintly. Like an alarm bell or some other sign of danger. "A fire? I have no idea what that's about."

Angie's voice slips past high-keyed into the well-tuned register of *don't you dare humiliate me*. "Well, I don't either. That's why you need to come and get it cleared up. The officer said someone reported your Jeep in the area during the night, right near where the vandalism happened."

"What store are you talking about?"

"A pet store, I think. On College Avenue."

That's when my ears begin to ring, loudly, a bright swelling of discord that mirrors my own confusion and drowns out Angie. Drowns out everything except my own recollection of the words Cate spoke to me the day after my date with Jenny.

things got kind of heated up there last night, didn't they?

"Mom, who called in the tip to the police?"

"They didn't tell me that."

"Was it Cate?"

"Don't use that tone with me, James."

"Was it?" I whisper.

"I don't know."

"I didn't *do* anything. Whatever it was, I didn't do it."

There's a pause.

"Mom? You believe me, right?"

She sighs. Deeply. "All I know is I can't go through this again. I can't. Neither can your father. So you need to fix whatever this is. You need to—"

I hang up on her.

In the silence that follows I'm unable to move. Or reluctant to. Maybe it's the thought of the stunned look on Angie's face or the fact that she's more worried about her own mental state than she is about believing in me, but either way, for what seems like forever, I stand sculpture-still in the middle of the woods as rain streams down my face and from my eyes.

I could stay like this all night, I think. Inertia suits me. The prior righteousness that fueled the rush to dig up my sister's secrets now feels more like folly than relief. I'm no match for Cate in mind or motive. I don't know how she does it or why, but she's always one step ahead of me. For all I know, her setting me up with the cops about this pet store thing could be her twisted way of asking for my help. That would be Cate logic all the way.

Eventually, I force myself into motion and begin the long walk back out of the woods. My legs feel weak, drained, and it's a good twenty minutes before I reach the spot of road where I left Dr. No. By the time I get there, darkness has settled over the valley, and the rain's trailed to a soft drizzle that makes it feel like God's spitting on me, or on everyone really, since nature's not something I like to take personally. I walk around to the back side of the Jeep and lift the hatch with a groan. I go to heave the messenger bag inside, right next to Cate's offending window-breaking brick, and that's when I see it.

I pause and blink. Bunched up and wadded into a corner by the wheel well is a crumpled plastic garbage bag. Inconspicuous enough, only . . . only it's not *mine*.

I lean forward onto my stomach to grab for it. My guess is that those auto body guys left their trash in here. Or more likely, given the way they sneered at me, it's a bag full of fecal matter or used hypodermic needles. But when I look inside, what I find is an assortment of prescription pill bottles, a handful of jewelry, including gold, pearls, what look like the-real-deal diamonds, some work gloves, a crowbar, an empty box of M-80 firecrackers, a book of gas station matches, and two articles of clothing—my missing khakis from my Friday-night date with Jenny and a faded Sayrebrook jazz band sweatshirt, both carrying the strong stench of gunpowder and smoke.

I grab on to the bumper and twist around to lean my butt against it. The plastic bag remains gripped in my left hand.

I stare at it, disbelieving. Someone put this here. Someone broke into my car and put this here.

Right?

I take gulping gasps of air.

Shit.

Shit.

Shit.

FORTY-EIGHT

My decision's made in a split second. I leap from the Jeep, slam the trunk closed with everything inside, then bolt across the road again. This time, I run right up the Ramirez ranch drive, past the horses and the rebuilt barn, and straight on toward the guest cottage. I'm not worried about being seen. I'm worried about Cate and I'm worried about me, and there's only one person on this earth who knows my sister better than I do.

Danny.

I want to talk to him.

I *need* to.

My lungs burn, but I push on.

This is either a fool's errand or a hero's quest.

As I approach the guest cottage, a whimper of relief escapes me. The lights are on, and Danny's white pickup's parked up against a redwood tree. I run faster. It's not only the thought of help that overwhelms me. It's the not being alone in all this.

The rain's tapered off, but water pools along the night-darkened ground. The combination of poor vision and damp stiff clothes means I barely make the leap from the ground up the narrow stairs to the redwood deck without falling ass over teakettle. I skid, steady myself, then rush to the French doors and pound on the glass.

No answer.

I pound more. I press my nose against the pane. The entire living space is visible, lit up by a wagon-wheel chandelier that hangs over the center of the room. Each of the individual bulbs glows like a lit torch, sending multicolored flares through the rain-streaked glass, but there's no movement from inside. Gritting my teeth, I yank the door handle.

It opens with a low creak.

I take a tentative step in. I cup my hands together and stage-whisper, "Danny?"

Nothing.

I say it louder. "Danny!"

My voice echoes back at me, but nothing else. I gird myself and walk all the way inside, skirting the unfolded futon and plush cream rug. My knee knocks against an end table. It wobbles, but manages to stay upright.

In the kitchen area things are more puzzling. A cracked ceramic plate with crumbs on it sits beside the sink, along with a half-empty bottle of Corona. I grab the beer. The bottle's almost full, and the glass is still cold.

Strange.

I take a quick look in the bathroom, which is the only space that's separate from the rest of the cottage, but the door's open and the light's off. Danny's simply not here.

But he can't be far. Perhaps he's visiting up at the main house or got called down to the barn.

Thud-whack!

I gasp and twist around.

Thud-whack!

I jump again, but it's only the French door. I didn't secure it when I came in, so now the black night wind's pushing it around, banging it against the frame, like something outside wants to get in real bad. Air slides from my lungs in relief. I steal a glance at the thick white rug. And freeze.

Large wet footprints cover the floor. Brown, sopping ones. Ones that weren't there before.

They definitely weren't.

Heart pounding and hands tingling, my gaze follows their path. The footprints go all the way across the room, past the rug, the end table, the futon.

Straight to me.

I look down.

At my own mud-caked boots.

I start to tremble. A creeping sense of doubt crawls up my spine to nest in the darkest nodes of my cortex. It's a familiar feeling, dizzying and homespun and irrepressible. Like an itch I can't scratch. Like a thought I can't silence. Like a—

A sharp buzzing gets my attention. My head swivels to see Danny's phone—it's on vibrate, which makes it jitter around on the kitchen counter where he left it. I reach over and grab it.

The screen informs me that there's a new text from someone named August. I don't know if that's a guy or a girl. The message reads, *look asshole you coming tonight or what?* so my instincts say guy, although I always thought girls were the ones named after months.

I scroll through the other apps on the home page, eager for information, for anything. Other than the fact that his wallpaper is a photo of him and Cate from high school, the only thing out of the ordinary that I see is in the call log. Danny's made a ton of outgoing calls to the same number recently. More than a ton. Ten times in one hour.

I hit redial.

The phone rings and rings and rings. No voice mail picks up. Nothing.

I hang up.

I stare at the call log some more. Then I pull my own phone out and dial the exact same number.

Cate answers on the first ring.

"Hey, little brother," she says. "Guess I know where to find you now, don't I?"

FORTY-NINE

I lock my knees to keep from falling. The tone in Cate's voice is so on the nose it hurts. It's sprite or tart or any of those words people use when they mean to say a girl's astute, but don't want to give her too much credit. But I don't underestimate my sister. Not one bit. In her brightness and cheer, what I pick up is threatening undertone and the final arrival of a long-brewing storm.

Cate's all about subtext.

"What's going on?" I ask, as my gaze darts from the stormy night to the swinging French door back to my dirty boots, that triad of dread I can't yet piece together.

"Why, hello to you, too," she purrs.

"You—you're setting me up, aren't you? You're trying to get me in trouble."

It's like I can hear her smirking through the phone. "Are you *mad* at me, Jamie?"

"No! I'm not mad. I'm confused. The cops want to talk to me about some fire. They think . . . they think *I* did it."

"Did you?"

I take a deep breath and think back to the bag in the Jeep. The firecrackers. The stolen jewelry. My own smoke-stained clothing.

The way I forget things.

"I d-don't know," I whisper.

She laughs. "So naturally you want to blame me. Figures. How's Danny, by the way? You can tell him to stop calling. I'm not interested."

"Danny's not here."

"But you have his phone?"

"Yeah, I do. I have *your* stuff, too, you know. I went and dug it all up this afternoon."

"My stuff? I don't know what you're talking about."

"The messenger bag you hid in the tree trunk after the fire. Remember that? With your journal and those books from Dr. Waverly's office and our mom's stone tiger. And *your* phone. I have that, too."

There's a long pause. "Hold on. *You* have all that?"

"Yeah. And Cate, the owl in Dr. Waverly's office. That was our mom's, too, wasn't it?"

"Of course it was."

"How did she get it?"

"Maybe I gave it to her as a fucking Christmas present. Maybe I didn't want to keep it hidden in a box in the back of my closet just to preserve poor Angie's sobby feelings any longer. Hold on, did you say there was *a phone*? What phone?"

"The phone you used to lure Sarah Ciorelli into the barn that night." I shake my head. "You tried to *kill* her."

Cate sputters. "Where the hell did you find all of this?"

"What do you mean where? I'm the one who buried it."

"*You* did that? Why?"

"For you! So the cops wouldn't find it. So you wouldn't get in worse trouble than you already were! But I shouldn't have bothered because now you're trying to ruin me!"

"Oh, God," she says. "Oh, no. This is like . . . I don't even know. Wow."

"*Wow?* Are you drunk or something?"

"No, I'm not drunk. That is not what I am."

"What are you, then?"

"I'm sad. I'm really fucking sad right now."

My head hurts. "I don't get it. That's what the thing with the conversion disorder was about, right? You knew I felt guilty about hiding evidence, and that's why my hands go numb when I get upset."

"Is *that* what you think?"

"Um . . . yeah." '

"No, no, that's not right, Jamie. Your conversion disorder isn't about burying my shit."

"It's not?"

"Well, when did your hands first go numb?"

"They went numb when I was at school. With Scooter. It was when I heard about Sarah Ciorelli and the fire."

"Was that before or after you buried those things in the woods?"

I start to tremble. My whole body.

"Before," I say softly.

"That's right."

"I don't understand."

"I know that. We need to talk. In person."

"Why? So you can send the cops after me?"

"No. Not that. Not that at all." She tells me where she is.

I can't hold back any longer. "Did you kill her, Cate? Our mom? Is that what this is about?"

"Why would you ask me that?"

"Why would I *not*? You tried to kill Sarah. You gave me that play. *Electra*. The one where the girl ends up killing her own mom. It's like, you want me to know, but you don't want to say it!"

There's silence.

"Cate?"

"Did you actually *read* that play I gave you?" she asks.

"Part of it. Enough."

"Well, no, not enough. Because Electra doesn't kill her mother, dickhead."

"She doesn't?"

"No. She's an accomplice, but she doesn't do the actual killing."

"Then who does?"

"Orestes," Cate says. "Her goddamn brother."

There's horror and then there's this moment.

There's right now.

No. Don't listen to her. She's crazy. She hates you. She's luring you in for the kill.

"You still sure you want to know the truth, Jamie?" Cate asks.

Do I?

Is there still a choice?

FIFTY

Two years ago, on the day my hands first went numb, when the feathery wind catchers and weather-aged copper bells guided me through the woods and brought me to the clearing where my sister used to put schoolgirls into trances and smoke from a hookah, I'd felt the strangest sense of déjà vu.

Like a premonition.

Like I was chasing fate.

Tonight, however, as I scramble through the same clearing under the cover of night, in an effort to avoid anyone who might be out searching for the intruder who broke into the Ramirez family's guest cottage, I don't know what I feel.

Fear. Confusion. Betrayal.

Helplessly, hopelessly lost.

Spying a human-sized hole in the underbrush, I wedge myself between fallen branches and a few wet saplings. My breath comes in sick urgent heaves. In the distance, I make out what sounds like the Doppler wail of police sirens. Or maybe that's my paranoia again, playing tricks on my mind and crafting perception into whatever form will torment me the most.

I don't *have* to go to Cate, I tell myself. I don't have to do what she says. That's in my control. I could just go home. Stop taking her calls. Pretend she never existed. It's not like I've ever learned anything from her anyway. She's cryptic. She's maddening. Ambiguity's the devil's emotion, and it's all I feel around Cate. It's like wearing my skin inside out, being near her. I am that raw. That vulnerable.

I could walk away. Stop looking for answers. Go to Jenny, sweet Jenny.

Who's waiting for me.

I whimper, thinking of Jenny's warmth, her dry spark-on-tinder touch. The way I'm bolder and happier and freer when I'm with her.

The thing is, in the same way I can't stop questioning miracles, I can't stop looking for answers. That's my fatal flaw, I think.

I want to believe in answers.

I *need* to believe in whys.

For the second time today, I pull my hands from my pockets and hold them in front of my face. They're tingling something crazy, but whether that's from cataplexy or conversion or cold, I can't be sure.

"What's really wrong with you?" I whisper. "If it's not burying Cate's stuff in the woods that made you do this, then what is it?"

My hands still don't answer.

But deep down, I think I know.

After waiting for what seems an eternity, with sharp twigs jabbing into the seat of my pants and Cate's sense of urgency burning into my soul, I make my move. I creep from my hiding spot back toward the road, hidden beneath the clouds of this moonless night. I arrive at my Jeep unseen.

I slip behind the wheel.

I head off in search of answers I may not wish to find.

4

EPISTROPHY

FIFTY-ONE

Driving Dr. No up the dark winding Mount Diablo roads to where my sister waits, I feel more like an impostor than ever. Only I'm not sure whether I'm playing at being the good guy this time.

Or the villain.

I park in the empty lot of a campground just north of Rock City. The campsites are closed, but apparently my sister's found a way to stay here. She found it the way she always finds things, I suppose. Through deceit, manipulation, through offering herself up to the first lonely park ranger she stumbled upon.

I can only imagine.

The winter wind hits me with a sucker punch the moment I step outside. With the elevation change, the air is brutal. It's biting. It's bone cold. I circle the looping dirt trail, trudging around and around beneath night gloom and looming trees. The rain hasn't started up again, but everything feels dank, loose, and close to melting. Moisture coats my eyelids, beads the bridge of my nose.

My seeking takes on a sense of desperation. My sister's not where I expect her to be. She's not in any of the numbered campsites. She's not in the ranger's trailer, which is set off from the main campground and appears to be empty. I find an old pink and yellow Honda scooter shoved off the roadside into a brambly thicket of blackberries, but when I call Cate's name, there's no response. I call out again, and I'm on the verge of breaking down under the weight of my own questions, when a familiar scent hits my nostrils.

Smoke.

My heart lurches and my hands die. Just like that, I'm disarmed, helpless, but still I follow the scent, sharp and burning. I have to. I move fast up the mountain, sidewinding over slick rock like a dog after a lure, single-minded and nose to ground. There's a second nesting of caves up here, ones steeper and more dangerous than those at Rock City. Ones with no name.

This is where I find her.

Cate stands on the edge of the craggy cliff, all skimpy clothes and cigarette blazing. Her knees bump dangerously against the stone retaining wall that's meant to keep people from slipping over, and her dark hair, lit up by the fire crackling in the cave behind her, whips and puffs in the blowing wind. It spreads out wide, like a cobra's hood. Her back is to me, but she knows I'm here.

She always knows.

I force myself to walk along the narrow path, heading straight for her. I am cautious, and I am scared. This is as far outside the chords as I've ever played. But somehow it *feels* right.

It feels like destiny.

As I approach, Cate turns. We stare at each other. The fireglow strikes her and she's not screaming at me this time or throwing bricks, so at last, I am able to take her in.

My sister is smeared eye makeup. She's bare feet and bruised legs in winter. She is fucking beautiful, and she is utter madness.

She's Cate.

After all this time.

"Oh, Jamie," she says, and I start to cry.

"I'm sorry," I say. "I don't even know what I did. But I'm so sorry."

She reaches out and wraps her arms around me in a way she hasn't done in years. In a way nobody's done in years. It's maternal in the most tragic of senses—like she wants to use her body to protect me from the wind, the elements, the harsh realities of the world.

Like she'd do anything to save me.

Maybe that's been her fatal flaw all along.

Protecting me from myself.

"You know, don't you?" she whispers in my ear.

I nod. I'm embarrassed to be crying, but now that I've started I can't stop. Emotion spills from me, twined with grief and fear and mostly fear. "I know I did something bad. Something that has to do with our mom. Nothing else makes sense. But I don't know what it is. Help me remember. Please."

Cate holds me tighter. "You're sure?"

"I'm sure."

She looks down. "Your hands. Are they—"

"Yes, they're numb."

She nods. "Once I tell you, you can't go back, you know."

"I know that. But please, tell me everything."

"Okay," she says. "Come sit by the fire, then. And listen."

I let her help me into the cave.

I let her help me sit down.

I close my eyes.

I try and hold on.

FIFTY-TWO

My sister's voice is all goose feathers and hard truth. In her Cate way, in language peppered with *fucks* and *assholes* and *goddamn cocksuckers*, she tells a tale that starts with "once upon a time." It's the tale of a golden-haired girl, one who lived alone with her two beloved children—a boy with a grim owlish nature and a girl as sleek, slippery, and cool as a pussycat.

It's also a sad tale, what Cate tells me. Maybe a cautionary one, too. I'm not sure. The girl in Cate's story had no money and she lived in a basement in the shadow of an oil refinery, on the bad side of a depressed town. She loved her children, Cate says, but love wasn't enough in her world. Money was what mattered, and so the girl worked three jobs and left her children with her upstairs neighbor when she was gone. The owlish boy hated this. He was colicky and sad, right from the start. No one could soothe him, and his early days were spent screaming in a barred wooden cage called a playpen, while the neighbor's Great Dane barked and barked, right in his face.

As the boy grew, his sadness grew with him. Only his sorrow evolved, spinning into something different, something darker, something quiet and cutting and sometimes cruel. At school when he was mad, he would hurt other children. He hurt his teacher, too. Cate says he always cried about it after, but after was always too late. Eventually his school didn't want him, and this broke his mother's heart. She didn't have the money or the power to convince them that five-year-olds deserved second chances. That what he needed was help.

Not punishment.

Or shame.

Cate says an evening came soon after when the golden-haired girl had to go to work, and the boy wanted her to stay. So he dumped milk all over her shirt. On purpose. The girl went to go change, but it was the boy's seven-year-old sister who became angry this time. She was sick of his tantrums and his problems, and she slapped him right across the face! Hard.

Cate says that for once, the boy didn't scream or hit back. Instead he slunk from the room while his sister cleaned up the milk. Moments later, she heard a gunshot coming from the bedroom they shared. Then another. Cate tells me she ran as fast as she could, terrified the boy had found the gun their mother kept for protection and shot himself. Instead what she found was her baby brother, alive, with the gun clutched in his tiny talon hands, and the golden-haired girl lying on the floor in front of him. Beneath her stretched a pool of blood as dark and rich as rubies.

Cate tells me that for one shining instant, her little brother was smug. Pleased with what he'd done.

And then he wasn't.

Then he cried out for his lost mother, a sick, broken, babyish sort of sound, and his sister felt so *guilty,* hitting him the way she had. When the cops and the coroner and the social workers came, she whispered that it had all been an accident, a terrible accident, and if they didn't exactly believe her, well, they didn't ask any more questions because there wasn't anyone left to ask. The boy wouldn't talk, and when they were finally alone, in the darkness of night, his sister held him in her lap and whispered in his ear.

She would take care of him, she promised.

She would keep him safe, she promised.

She would never let anyone find out the truth, she promised.

Ever.

Then, Cate tells me, she folded her arms around me and held me close, so close, until I almost stopped breathing. Until all I heard was the soft beating of her heart. A sound that was rhythmic.

Soothing.

Hypnotic.

FIFTY-THREE

There are some dreams you can't wake up from. These are the dreams that try and trick you. The ones that lull you into believing you're awake, that your eyes are open and your mind knows what it's doing. But it's a lie. In reality, you're paralyzed. And when something terrible comes for you, you can't move.

No matter what you do.

No matter how hard you try.

The story my sister tells is not a nice one.

It is not a dream I want to be having.

But it's *mine*.

I can't escape it.

FIFTY-FOUR

When I open my eyes, I'm sitting with Cate in the cave with my back hunched against the sharp rocky wall. My bones are still cold. My hands are still dead.

I absorb her words. Slowly. I probe around in my mind and my heart for any hint of recollection. Of understanding.

Could I really have done what she's saying? Killed my own mother in a fit of rage . . . out of spite?

It doesn't feel right, this version of the truth. It's like trying on a stranger's skin or waking up in a land whose language makes you foreign, but given what I know about amnesia, I guess that's the point. Not remembering has a purpose. An empty mind can be filled with such palatable lies. And when I think of Darlene and Miss Louise, with their coy, careful words and sad, shifty looks, I realize perhaps there are some truths that nobody can handle, and which everyone is more than willing to forget.

But from one truth follows so many others. I don't need Cate to tell me that, and it's no feat of cognitive reasoning to deduce that if I've forgotten one dark shameful moment from my past, I've forgotten more. That for me, perhaps, forgetting isn't passive, but active—a means for me to flush my worst and weakest moments from my spotty mind like loose change or gum wrappers or anything else I can't bear to carry. That maybe nothing can bring those memories back. Not therapy. Not my sister's own impassioned attempts at hypnosis.

Nothing.

"The barn," I say dully. "I did that, too, didn't I? And you took the blame?"

My sister nods.

"That's why my hands go numb. It's when I'm around you, right? Or when I feel guilty for setting the fire."

"Yes," she says. "That's what I think, anyway."

"But *why*? Why would I do that?"

"I don't know why. I always thought you were mad at Hector for something. Or Danny even. But tonight, after hearing about this phone you dug up, maybe it was Sarah all along, huh?"

"Sarah?" I say. Again it feels wrong. But in the way the ocean tide rolls out to reveal the life thriving beneath the waves, as I force myself to think back, it's the memory of those texts I found on the throwaway cell phone that brings clarity. Those awful, incriminating texts, the ones I'd always thought my sister had sent but had never really understood.

hey sarah.
look out your window
hope you're not slow

better be fast
better hurry
better
run.

The voice inside my head is stern now, disapproving. It says, *Cate may not know why you did it, but you know, don't you? You hated her. You always hated her,* and my shoulders droop and my heart sinks, because the voice is right. I *did* hate Sarah. The way she mocked and bossed me. The way she looked down on me and made me feel small. I'd wanted her out of my life. Scooter's, too.

She made me very, very angry.

And I don't like to be angry.

I look up at Cate, her gaunt face, her haunted eyes.

"You're not going to do that passing out thing, are you?" she says sharply.

"N-no. I don't think so. I think . . . I think I'm in shock, maybe. But you're right. What you said about Sarah."

She doesn't answer.

"I'm sorry," I say. "It's not enough. But I am."

Cate squares her jaw. "I'm sorry, too. I mean, I came back here because I wanted to *hurt* you. I wanted to see if I could set you off. But I didn't have to confess to the fire, back then. No one made me. It just felt like a way to atone for what I'd done all those years ago. A way to make me feel less crazy. Only once I was locked up, there was no grace. No absolution, like they tell you in church. It was just . . . awful. So I wanted you to feel a little bit of that awfulness, too. Even if you didn't remember why."

"I deserve to feel a lot worse than that."

"No, you don't. Hearing tonight about how you tried to protect me by burying that bag, not knowing what you'd done, well, hell, it reminded me that you're not a bad person. Just sick. Very, very sick. But you're still my owl. You're still in pain. And I'm still your sister. Crazy Cate."

I shake my head. What else can I do? I can't say anything to that. What I've done, who I am, it's indefensible.

Her voice softens. "You know, the story I wanted you to read in that book wasn't *Electra*."

"What was it?"

"Antigone."

Of course. The one I haven't read.

"What's it about?" I ask.

"It's about a girl who stands up for what she believes is right. A girl who stands up for her brother."

"What happens to her?"

"She dies. On her terms."

I crumple then. I'm crushed. I can't look at my sister anymore, because I'm lost, drowning, swallowed up by the misery of it all. By the way that there's tragic and tragedy, and the fact that our lives have been both all at once. Without me even knowing it. Deep down, I'm stupid, I guess. Or blind. Maybe, like Oedipus, I've always been blind—believing I can understand the ways of the world. But there's no outsmarting fate, and there are no miracles to question. The past is what matters, and it's the one thing that can never be changed.

No matter how badly you want to.

No matter how hard you try.

"You're not crazy," I tell Cate.

"Oh, I don't know about that."

"You're not," I insist. "You're my sister."

"That'll do it," she says, and somehow we're both able to smile.

"I have something to show you before I go." She reaches and pulls an item from her purse. Holds it in front of me.

It's a photograph. I lean forward to see it better, but it's a portrait of a young woman. She's almost a child, really. And she's beaming like the sun. Her blond hair falls into her face. She's gazing down at a baby swathed in blue.

"Cate," I whimper. "Is that—"

"It is," she says. "And you."

My chest knots up, shortening my breath. "She's beautiful."

"Yeah, she was. She really was. I had another photo, too, but the goddamn rain ruined it."

"Don't go," I say quickly. "Danny still loves you."

"I know he does. I was with him the night of the fire, before I saw you sneak in, reeking of smoke. He never believed I set it, and he waited all this time. But . . ."

"But what?"

Cate pushes her lips into one of her enigmatic smiles. "But I have what I need right now, and it's not love."

My heart aches. Like that night in her room all those years ago, before she walked herself into a courtroom to be sentenced for something she was innocent of, something I'd done, I am losing my sister. Again.

She touches my cheek. "Promise me you'll get help, Jamie. You'll be an asshole if you don't."

I give a hoarse laugh. "You think they'll help me in jail when I get arrested for that pet store fire?"

"You won't get arrested. I already called back and gave the cops about twenty other license plates. They know I'm a hoax. They don't have any evidence."

"But I did it."

She blinks. "Oh." Then: *"Oh."*

"Yeah."

"Get help," Cate repeats firmly. Then she leans forward, reaching for the photograph resting on my lap.

"Don't take that," I say. "Please."

"This is the one thing I can't give up. It's all I have of her. I'm sorry." With a rueful look, Cate plucks the faded picture from me and slips it into her purse. Then she uncrosses her legs and reaches for her shoes, which sit beside her. My heart beats very fast. My dead hands tingle. Faintly. Like an omen. Or a warning.

I want that photograph.

Pressure builds inside me, volcanic strength. Only what's growing inside me might be hotter. More powerful. More explosive.

I want that photograph.

Cate uses the tip of her finger to wedge one of her shoes over her heel. She reaches for her purse and goes to stand up. In a moment she'll be gone.

Forever.

It happens. My hands come back to life, and I lunge for Cate. She cries out when I grab for her, and twists her body. The movement catches me off guard. Wrapped together, we writhe and stumble out of the cave, into the night. We crash against the stone retaining wall. Cate's legs press against it, then her hips and her back. I'm pushing her. She starts to slip over, but won't let go. She fights back, clawing at me, kicking, punching, shouting, anything.

I fight harder.

I think

this is madness

I think

this is sick

I think

I won't let her beat me.

FIFTY-FIVE

There are some dreams you can't wake up from.
   Ever.
   These are called nightmares.

FIFTY-SIX

When I open my eyes, I don't know where I am.

I'm outside. Alone. Walking down an empty road. Trees surround me, and everything is black. It's night, and the air swirls with a howling wind and thick rolls of low-lying ground fog. I've got a jacket on, but it's not enough. My teeth chatter. I tremble with each step. My body feels bruised and stiff.

How did I get here?

My head spins. I feel dizzy, so I stop walking. I look around. I don't see the Jeep anywhere. There are houses on the hillside above me, resting on stilts and pressing into the earth. Their lights are all off.

It must be late.

Very late.

I don't know where I am.

Or why I'm here.

I'm scared.

I pull my phone out of my jacket pocket. It's 12:38 A.M. There are a bunch of text messages, all from Jenny. Seeing these gives me a burst of excitement, of brilliant anticipation, but there are other feelings mixed in there, too. Like sorrow.

Like shame.

I feel heavy with shame, but I don't know why.

I scroll to the phone log, searching for more clues. For more evidence. I've got a lot of missed calls and voice mails, but a few from earlier in the day are from a blocked number. And that's when I remember.

Cate.

I close my eyes very tightly. Something is wrong with my memory, it feels scattered, elusive, but I know the pieces are there, inside of me, so I force myself to focus.

You went to see her. She had something to tell you about your mother. About you.

My mother.

It comes back to me then, the whole evening, like a shuttle coming down from space, landing hard and fast, on the edge of burning up. Remembering hurts. The images are hazy, this eclipse of the past and the truth, but in my mind's eye I see myself driving up to the mountain. Walking around the campground and finding my sister by fire scent. It's like watching a movie or Plato's allegory come to life, seeing myself sit across from Cate, shadows flickering on the cave wall. Her mouth moves, and she talks and talks.

I know what she's telling me.

I killed my own mother.

Cate's telling me other things, too. Like how there's something sick and broken about my brain. How it can make me forget things that I do when I'm angry. Very bad things.

I am a bad person.

There's more inside of me even my sister doesn't know about, I think. Like how I set a fire at the church in the hope she'd get blamed for it. Like how I broke into neighborhood houses and stole stuff as a way to set her up. I *did* do those things, right? What other explanation is there? Even worse, Cate gave me credit for burying the messenger bag in the woods in an effort to save her. But when I think about it more, I realize that if I was the one who hid evidence of the fire inside the bag with her belongings in the first place, then I'm probably the one who did other things, too, like calling in the anonymous tip to the cops or setting her up online. So although my conscious mind may have tried to save my sister, my subconscious wanted to frame her. Meaning the person I was *really* saving all along was . . . myself. This makes me calculating.

Manipulative.

Cowardly.

Cate, where are you?

I need your help.

Please.

Only Cate doesn't answer, and I don't know where she is. My last memory is of her showing me a photograph of our mother. Of me wanting to keep it.

And of her telling me no.

What happens after that is black. I don't and can't remember.

My stomach twists. A wave of sickness threatens to overwhelm me, but I don't give in to it. I can't. I'm not helpless. I have choices still, don't I? I have ways to right my wrongs. Or at least *try*. I owe it to everyone I've hurt to do that. So I should call Dr. Waverly. That would be a start. I could explain to her what happened and what I know. I could ask her to please, please help me. She understands about the amnesia, that something might be wrong with my brain and how I remember things. She wrote about it in the margins of her book. Plus she genuinely cares about me. I know she does. Even Cate trusted her, in her own way. Giving her the stone owl that hurt Angie too much to have around. Cate knew Dr. Waverly would set it somewhere I was guaranteed to see it. It's like my sister wanted a little piece of our mother watching over me.

Like she wanted me to *remember*.

My heart, it hurts.

So much.

I want to die. I don't know what else to do.

I cannot stand the pain.

Cate, wherever you are, whatever I've done. I'm sorry. I'm so sorry. You've been the strong one all this time. The one with courage. You don't deserve a brother like me. You deserve better.

You gave and I took.

I lift my head, and that's when I see it—a mule deer is in the road, not ten feet away from where I am.

I stare at the animal, and she stares back. Time ticks by. Moonglow lights her coat, which is bright and gold and fills me with the sort of warmth and love I want so badly to believe is real.

Mom, I think madly. *I love you.*

I take one step forward, and the animal comes to life, a doe in flight. She bounds swiftly into the darkness.

Heart pounding, I do what I have to—I follow her. The doe's path leads me into the black night that has swallowed her up. The ominous creak of the trees above sets my nerves on edge as I pick my way across the ground littered with wind-felled branches. I stumble but keep going. Soon, I find myself looking over the edge of a steep canyon.

Vast. Gaping.

An endless abyss.

I can't imagine the doe leaped this way knowingly. It'd be a death sentence, for sure. Maybe it was just an illusion. Maybe she simply left my line of vision before bolting down the side of the road, small white tail flipping behind her.

My mind swirls with maybes.

A strong gust of wind comes up from behind, shoving me closer to the edge. I grind my heels into the dirt as the groan of branches overhead intensifies. I squeeze my eyes shut, and still, *still,* I can't remember my own mother. My mind's too clouded by sweet, sweet scents and dark-haired lies. All I have that's real inside of me is Angie. Eternally grieving Angie. Some pair we've made, all these years: the mother who can't let go of the past.

And me, who can't seem to hold on.

When I open my eyes again, I'm staring into the yawning descent, the sheer drop down, the utter blackness. I wonder what it would feel like to fly. I think of Richard Wright, his grit, his passion, his hunger.

His strength.

I have none of it. I have nothing but self-loathing. Losing memories to trauma is one thing. But doing it willfully and making up new ones. That's *aberrant.* Dangerously so.

I'm sorry, Jenny.

I bend my legs.

I protest this fraud.

FIFTY-SEVEN

There are some dreams you *do* wake up from, only to find you can't remember them at all.

But that doesn't mean these dreams don't matter. That their epistrophic wisdom isn't playing inside of you, over and over and over again. Somewhere. Somehow. Charting your course in ways you aren't even aware of. Marching you straight toward suffering or glory.

These are the dreams that can make you feel sad when you should be happy.

These are the dreams that hold our most private of truths.

These are the dreams that destinies are made of.

FIFTY-EIGHT

When I open my eyes, I am sitting at a piano in the dark with Jenny by my side.

My awareness surfaces slowly, like emerging from the cool depths of the most serene mountain lake. We are in her living room, alone, with a fire crackling in the fireplace. Candles illuminate the large family portrait hanging on the wall above me. The portrait includes a young man who must be Jenny's brother, the one who got himself locked up for good. I'm intrigued, but don't stare for too long because my neck hurts. In fact, my whole body feels bone-tired, like maybe I've just walked a hundred miles or even a hundred more. There's music in the air, something dark and twisted, and when I look down, I see that I'm playing a song for Jenny. It's Monk, of course, but not "Evidence," which I'm kind of sick of.

No, it's "Misterioso."

My mind follows where my hands go. I lean into the music. I hit the offbeats at all the right times. I stretch my fingers and reach for the keys, pounding out the melody, the chords, the haunting dissonance, and for the first time in a long while, the muscles in my hands feel strong. Trustworthy. Sure of themselves. Jenny, who's dressed in nothing but a nightgown and robe, has both her arms wrapped around my waist, and when I'm done playing she wipes tears I didn't even know were there from my eyes.

"That was beautiful," she whispers, and I want to ask her things like:

what am I doing?

how did I get here?

where have I been?

But these things are embarrassing to ask, and so I say nothing because I'm shy and I like Jenny, and I don't want her to stop liking me.

"Thank you," I whisper back, and then she's leaning her head against my chest and holding me tighter. I understand that she's comforting me. That she wants me not to cry or be upset anymore, only I don't know what I might be upset about. I mean, I'm here. With her.

It's all that I want.

"Thank you," I murmur again. "For everything."

"I had no idea your sister was so sick. I hope the cops find her. Get her help, you know? Real help."

I nod.

"Has she been suicidal before?"

"Yes," I say, but is this true? I don't know. The word just pops out of my mouth, like it's got a mind of its own.

Jenny's rubbing my shoulders now. It feels good. "You're brave for trying to find her on your own. After what she did."

Brave. That's a funny way to describe me. I am not brave. I'm nice.

Right now I'm other things, too, because I want more of that good feeling I get when Jenny touches me.

"Thank you for coming over, anyway," she says. "For keeping your promise."

"Of course," I say, and I kiss her.

That's when the rest of the world vanishes. Jenny and I come together, our bodies, our minds, and I lose myself in her, in who she is and what she means. Soon all I know of myself, my surroundings, is warm girl, soft skin, the sweet rub and burn of desire. My nerves are tingling, only not in a bad way, and I don't feel it in my hands now. This is a tingling that comes from within, moving through my stomach, my gut, down even farther. I breathe faster. Harder. Everything but this moment melts from my mind like snowpack.

We move from sitting up to lying down, from the piano bench to the floor in front of the fire where there are blankets and pillows already laid out, waiting for us. We grope and paw and roll around. There is a sense of abandon in everything we do, a sense of freedom. My lips travel from Jenny's mouth to the smooth nape of her neck. They dance across her skin and down her spine. Warm butterfly brushes.

Her robe comes off. Then my jacket. The fire cracks and burns. There's more heat. More desire. Jenny is bold. She pulls her gown up and pushes my hands down her body. She wants me to touch her. Everywhere.

She makes happy noises when I do.

"Jamie," she says.

"Mmm?"

"This feels really good."

"I'm glad."

"Do you want to . . . ?"

"Yes," I say breathlessly. "I do."

She slides my shirt over my head, then reaches down to tug my jeans over my hips. I let her. I'm too dazed to be of much help, too entranced by her body and the hypnotic sway of her breasts as she moves, alluring softness lit by fireglow. This whole thing's like a dream, and I'm wondering if she knows it's my first time and that I think it's absolutely perfect. But I'm also wondering about these bruises on my arms and chest. I glance down, confused about where they came from. They *hurt*. My ribs especially. And that's when Jenny says softly, "What's this?"

I look up. She's got something in her hands. A photograph.

"I don't know," I say. "What is it?"

"It was in the back pocket of your pants."

My pants? That's weird. I take the photo from her hand and look closer. The print is old, faded. It's a picture of a woman with hair that's the same blond shade as Jenny's, and she's holding an infant. I've never seen it before.

"I don't know what that is," I say again.

"I thought it might have something to do with, you know, your real mom."

I laugh. That's an odd thing to say. There are no pictures of my birth mom and there never have been. That's what Angie's always told me. Not one trace of my mother's existence remains on this earth, except for me. And Cate. But Cate's the last person I want to think about right now, what with her phone calls and her threats of throwing herself off a cliff. Thinking about her makes me sad, and I don't want to be sad tonight. I'm already the kind of person who's sad a lot.

So I take the photograph, crumple it, and toss it into the fire. Smoke flares, then fades. It feels good to do this. Like I'm in control for once.

I turn back to Jenny. She watches me with curious eyes.

"It was nothing," I tell her, and I push her hair back so that I can see the mole on her throat, that hint of darkness surrounded by so much light. "Nothing important. I'd remember if it was."

ACKNOWLEDGMENTS

Many thanks to Michael Bourret and Sara Goodman for their ongoing support and for always helping me find my way; to Jessica Preeg, Anne Marie Tallberg, Jeanne Marie Hudson, Elizabeth Catalano, Stephanie Davis, Kerri Resnick, Talia Sherer, and the whole St. Martin's team for being so kind and brilliant; and to Phoebe North, Corrine Jackson, Kate Hart, Sarah Enni, Kody Keplinger, Veronica Roth, Lee Bross, Kirsten Hubbard, Kristin Halbrook, Kari Olson, Brandy Colbert, Will Kuehn, and Dr. Lin for their vast wisdom and eternal encouragement. Special heartfelt gratitude to my long-ago bass teacher, Clark Suprynowicz, for sharing his passion for both jazz and *Antigone*;

and to my dear friends Scott Bruner (owner of the original Dr. No) and Mieka Strawhorn for always making me laugh.

Lastly, thank you to my family, in all its forms. You're a part of me, whether I know it or not.